HORRID HENRY'S BIG BUMPER BOOK

Originally published separately as *Horrid Henry's Big Bad Book*
and *Horrid Henry's Wicked Ways*
by Orion Children's Books
a division of the Orion Publishing Group Ltd
Orion House
5 Upper Saint Martin's Lane
London WC2H 9EA

This edition published 2009 for Index Books Ltd

A catalogue record for this book is available
from the British Library.

Printed in India

21
36
15
79
16
27
36
39
---
219 X

3

CONTENTS

CONTENTS

HORRID HENRY'S NEW TEACHER

'Now Henry,' said Dad. 'Today is the first day of school. A chance for a fresh start with a new teacher.'

'Yeah, yeah,' scowled Horrid Henry.

He hated the first day of term. Another year, another teacher to show who was boss. His first teacher, Miss Marvel, had run screaming from the classroom after two weeks. His next teacher, Mrs Zip, had run screaming from the classroom after one day. Breaking in new teachers wasn't easy, thought Henry, but someone had to do it.

Dad got out a piece of paper and waved it.

'Henry, I never want to read another school report like this again,' he said. 'Why can't your school reports be like Peter's?'

Henry started whistling.

'Pay attention, Henry,' shouted Dad. 'This is important. Look at this report.'

HENRY'S SCHOOL REPORT

It has been horrible Teaching Henry this year. He is rude, lazy and disruptive. The worst student I have ever taught.

Behaviour: Horrid

English: Horrid

Maths: Horrid

Science: Horrid

P.E: Horrid

'What about *my* report?' said Perfect Peter.

Dad beamed.

'Your report was perfect, Peter,' said Dad. 'Keep up the wonderful work.'

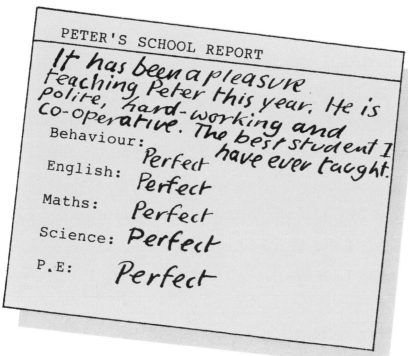

PETER'S SCHOOL REPORT

It has been a pleasure teaching Peter this year. He is polite, hard-working and co-operative. The best student I have ever taught.

Behaviour: Perfect

English: Perfect

Maths: Perfect

Science: Perfect

P.E: Perfect

Peter smiled proudly.

'You'll just have to try harder, Henry,' said Peter, smirking.

Horrid Henry was a shark sinking his teeth into a drowning sailor.

'OW W W W,' shrieked Peter. 'Henry bit me!'

'Don't be horrid, Henry!' shouted Dad. 'Or no TV for a week.'

'I don't care,' muttered Henry. When he became king he'd make it a law that parents, not children, had to go to school.

Horrid Henry pushed and shoved his way into class and grabbed the seat next to Rude Ralph.

'Nah nah ne nah nah, I've got a new football,' said Ralph.

Henry didn't have a football. He'd kicked his through Moody Margaret's window.

'Who cares?' said Horrid Henry.

The classroom door slammed. It was Mr Nerdon, the toughest, meanest, nastiest teacher in the school.

'SILENCE!' he said, glaring at them with his bulging eyes. 'I don't want to hear a sound. I don't even want to hear anyone breathe.'

The class held its breath.

'GOOD!' he growled. 'I'm Mr Nerdon.'

Henry snorted. What a stupid name.

'Nerd,' he whispered to Ralph.

Rude Ralph giggled.

'Nerdy Nerd,' whispered Horrid Henry, snickering.

Mr Nerdon walked up to Henry and jabbed his finger in his face.

'Quiet, you horrible boy!' said Mr Nerdon. 'I've got my eye on you. Oh yes. I've heard about your other teachers. Bah! I'm made of stronger stuff. There will be no nonsense in *my* class.'

We'll see about that, thought Henry.

'Our first sums for the year are on the board. Now get to work,' ordered Mr Nerdon.

Horrid Henry had an idea.

Quickly he scribbled a note to Ralph.

Ralph – I bet you that I can make Mr. Nerdon run screaming out of class by the end of lunchtime.

No way, Henry

If I do will you give me your new football?

O.K. But if you don't, you have to give me your pound coin.

O.K.

Horrid Henry took a deep breath and went to work. He rolled up some paper, stuffed it in his mouth, and spat it out. The spitball whizzed through the air and pinged Mr Nerdon on the back of his neck.

Mr Nerdon wheeled round.

'You!' snapped Mr Nerdon. 'Don't you mess with me!'

'It wasn't *me*!' said Henry. 'It was Ralph.'

'Liar!' said Mr Nerdon. 'Sit at the back of the class.'

Horrid Henry moved his seat next to Clever Clare.

'Move over, Henry!' hissed Clare. 'You're on my side of the desk.'

Henry shoved her.

'Move over yourself,' he hissed back.

Then Horrid Henry reached over and broke Clare's pencil.

'Henry broke my pencil!' shrieked Clare.

Mr Nerdon moved Henry next to Weepy William.

Henry pinched him.

Mr Nerdon moved Henry next to Tough Toby.

Henry jiggled the desk.

Mr Nerdon moved Henry next to Lazy Linda.

Henry scribbled all over her paper.

Mr Nerdon moved Henry next to Moody Margaret.

Moody Margaret drew a line down the middle of the desk.

'Cross that line, Henry, and you're dead,' said Margaret under her breath.

Henry looked up. Mr Nerdon was writing spelling words on the board.

Henry started to rub out Margaret's line.

'Stop it, Henry,' said Mr Nerdon, without turning around.

Henry stopped.

Mr Nerdon continued writing.

Henry pulled Margaret's hair.

Mr Nerdon moved Henry next to Beefy Bert, the biggest boy in the class.

Beefy Bert was chewing his pencil and trying to add 2 + 2 without much luck.

Horrid Henry inched his chair onto Beefy Bert's side of the desk.

Bert ignored him.

Henry poked him.
Bert ignored him.
Henry hit him.
POW!
The next thing
Henry knew
he was lying
on the floor,
looking up at
the ceiling.
Beefy Bert
continued chewing his pencil.

'What happened, Bert?' said Mr Nerdon.

'I dunno,' said Beefy Bert.

'Get up off the floor, Henry!' said Mr Nerdon.
A faint smile appeared on the
teacher's slimy lips.

'He hit me!' said
Henry. He'd
never
felt such
a punch
in his life.

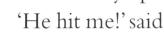

'It was an accident,' said Mr Nerdon. He smirked. 'You'll sit next to Bert from now on.'

That's it, thought Henry. Now it's war.

'How absurd, to be a nerdy bird,' said Horrid Henry behind Mr Nerdon's back.

Slowly Mr Nerdon turned and walked towards him. His hand was clenched into a fist.

'Since you're so good at rhyming,' said Mr Nerdon, 'everyone write a poem. Now.'

Henry slumped in his seat and groaned. A poem! Yuck! He hated poems. Even the word *poem* made him want to throw up.

Horrid Henry caught Rude Ralph's eye. Ralph was grinning and mouthing, 'A pound, a pound!' at him. Time was running out. Despite Henry's best efforts, Mr Nerdon still hadn't run screaming from the class. Henry would have to act fast to get that football.

What horrible poem could he write? Horrid Henry smiled. Quickly he picked up his pencil and went to work.

'Now, who's my first victim?' said Mr Nerdon. He looked round the room. 'Susan! Read your poem.'

Sour Susan stood up and read:

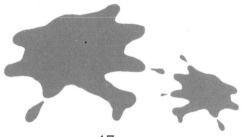

'Bow wow
Bow wow
Woof woof woof
I'm a dog, not a cat, so…
SCAT!'

'Not enough rhymes,' said Mr Nerdon. 'Next…' He looked round the room. 'Graham!'

Greedy Graham stood up and read:

'Chocolate chocolate chocolate sweet,
Cakes and doughnuts can't be beat.
Ice cream is my favourite treat
With lots and lots of pie to eat!'

'Too many rhymes,' said Mr Nerdon. 'Next…' He scowled at the class. Henry tried to look as if he didn't want the teacher to call on him.

'Henry!' snapped Mr Nerdon. 'Read your poem!'

Horrid Henry stood up and read:

'Pirates puke on stormy seas,
Giants spew on top of trees.'

Henry peeked at Mr Nerdon. He looked pale. Henry continued to read:

'Kings are sick in golden loos,
Dogs throw up on Daddy's shoes.'

Henry peeked again at Mr Nerdon. He looked green. Any minute now, thought Henry, and he'll be out of here screaming. He read on:

'Babies love to make a mess,
Down the front of Mum's best dress,
And what car ride would be complete,
Without the stink of last night's treat?'

'That's enough,' choked Mr Nerdon.

'Wait, I haven't got to the good bit,' said Horrid Henry.

'I said that's enough!' gasped Mr Nerdon. 'You fail.'

He made a big black mark in his book.

'I threw up on the boat!' shouted Greedy Graham.

'I threw up on the plane!' shouted Sour Susan.

'I threw up in the car!' shouted Dizzy Dave.

'I said that's enough!' ordered Mr Nerdon. He glared at Horrid Henry. 'Get out of here, all of you! It's lunchtime.'

Rats, thought Henry. Mr Nerdon was one tough teacher.

Rude Ralph grabbed him.

'Ha ha, Henry,' said Ralph. 'You lose. Gimme that pound.'

'No,' said Henry. 'I've got until the end of lunch.'

'You can't do anything to him between now and then,' said Ralph.

'Oh yeah?' said Henry. 'Just watch me.'

Then Henry had a wonderful, spectacular idea. This was it. The best plan he'd ever had. Someday someone would stick a plaque on the school wall celebrating Henry's genius. There would be songs written about him. He'd probably even get a medal. But first things first. In order for his plan to work to perfection, he needed Peter.

Perfect Peter was playing hopscotch with his friends Tidy Ted and Spotless Sam.

'Hey Peter,' said Henry. 'How would you like to be a real member of the Purple Hand?'

The Purple Hand was Horrid Henry's secret club. Peter had wanted to join for ages, but naturally Henry would never let him.

Peter's jaw dropped open.

'Me?' said Peter.

'Yes,' said Henry. 'If you can pass the secret club test.'

'What do I have to do?' said Peter eagerly.

'It's tricky,' said Henry. 'And probably much too hard for you.'

'Tell me, tell me,' said Peter.

'All you have to do is lie down right there below that window and stay absolutely still. You mustn't move until I tell you to.'

'Why?' said Peter.

'Because that's the test,' said Henry.

Perfect Peter thought for a moment.

'Are you going to drop something on me?'

'No,' said Henry.

'OK,' said Peter. He lay down obediently.

'And I need your shoes,' said Henry.

'Why?' said Peter.

Henry scowled.

'Do you want to be in the Purple Hand or not?' said Henry.

'I do,' said Peter.

'Then give me your shoes and be quiet,' said Henry. 'I'll be checking on you. If I see you moving one little bit you can't be in my club.'

Peter gave Henry his trainers, then lay still as a statue.

Horrid Henry grabbed the shoes, then dashed up the stairs to his classroom.

It was empty. Good.

Horrid Henry went over to the window and opened it. Then he stood there, holding one of Peter's shoes in each hand.

Henry waited until he heard Mr Nerdon's footsteps. Then he went into action.

'Help!' shouted Horrid Henry. 'Help!'

Mr Nerdon entered. He saw Henry and glowered.

'What are you doing here? Get out!'

'Help!' shouted Henry. 'I can't hold on to him much longer… he's slipping… aaahhh, he's fallen!'

Horrid Henry held up the empty shoes.

'He's gone,' whispered Henry. He peeked out of the window. 'Ugghh, I can't look.'

Mr Nerdon went pale. He ran to the window and saw Perfect Peter lying still and shoeless on the ground below.

'Oh no,' gasped Mr Nerdon.

'I'm sorry,' panted Henry. 'I tried to hold on to him, honest, I –'

'Help!' screamed Mr Nerdon. He raced down the stairs. 'Police! Fire! Ambulance! Help! Help!'

He ran over to Peter and knelt by his still body.

'Can I get up now, Henry?' said Perfect Peter.

'What!?' gasped Mr Nerdon. 'What did you say?'

Then the terrible truth dawned. He, Ninius Nerdon, had been tricked.

'YOU HORRID BOY! GO STRAIGHT TO THE HEAD TEACHER – NOW!' screeched Mr Nerdon.

Perfect Peter jumped to his feet.

'But… but –' spluttered Perfect Peter.

'Now!' screamed Mr Nerdon. 'How dare you! To the head!'

'AAAGGGHHHH,' shrieked Peter.

He slunk off to the head's office, weeping.

Mr Nerdon turned to race up the stairs to grab Henry.

'I'll get you, Henry!' he screamed. His face was white. He looked as if he were going to faint.

'Help,' squeaked Mr Nerdon.

Then he fainted.

Clunk! Thunk! Thud!

NEE NAW NEE NAW NEE NAW.

When the ambulance arrived, the only person lying on the ground was Mr Nerdon. They scooped him on to a stretcher and took him away.

The perfect end to a perfect day, thought Horrid Henry, throwing his new football in the air. Peter sent home in disgrace. Mr Nerdon gone for good. Even the news that scary Miss Battle-Axe would be teaching Henry's class didn't bother him. After all, tomorrow was another day.

HORRID HENRY'S FAVOURITE POEM

I'm Gonna Throw Up

Pirates puke on stormy seas
Giants spew on top of trees.
Kings are sick in golden loos
Dogs throw up on Daddy's shoes.

Babies love to make a mess
Down the front of Mum's best dress.
And what car ride would be complete
Without the stink of last night's treat?

Teachers who force kids to eat
Shepherd's pie with rancid meat
Can't be surprised when at their feet
The upchucked meal splats complete.

Rollercoasters, swirling cups
Can make anyone throw up.
Ferris wheels, icky sweets,
Pavement pizzas spray the streets.

Hats are handy when in town
Should your guts flip upside down.
A bag's a fine and private place
To avoid public disgrace
When, tummy heaving, insides peeling,
You suddenly get that awful feeling —
'Mum! I'm gonna throw up!'

If you're caught short while at sea
Don't worry! You'll die eventually.
But I for one do not believe
That bobbing ships cause folk to heave.
Sitting at the Captain's table
I scoffed as much as I was able.
I ate so many lovely dishes —
URGHHH! Now it's time to feed
the fishes.

HORRID HENRY'S NITS

Scratch. Scratch. Scratch.

Dad scratched his head.

'Stop scratching, please,' said Mum. 'We're eating dinner.'

Mum scratched her head.

'Stop scratching, please,' said Dad. 'We're eating dinner.'

Henry scratched his head.

'Stop scratching, Henry!' said Mum and Dad.

'Uh-oh,' said Mum. She put down her fork and frowned at Henry.

'Henry, do you have nits *again*?'

'Of course not,' said Henry.

'Come over to the sink, Henry,' said Mum.

'Why?' said Henry.

'I need to check your head.'

Henry dragged his feet over to her as slowly as possible. It's not fair, he thought. It wasn't his fault nits loved him. Henry's head was a gathering place for nits far and wide. They probably held nit parties there and foreign nits visited him on their holidays.

Mum dragged the nit comb across Henry's head. She made a face and groaned.

'You're crawling with nits, Henry,' said Mum.

'Ooh, let's see,' said Henry. He always liked counting how many nits he had.

'One, two, three … forty-five, forty-six, forty-seven …' he counted, dropping them on to a paper towel.

'It's not polite to count nits,' said his younger brother, Perfect Peter, wiping his mouth with his spotless napkin, 'is it, Mum?'

'It certainly isn't,' said Mum.

Dad dragged the nit comb across his head and made a face.

'Ughh,' said Dad.

Mum dragged the comb through her hair.

'Bleeeech,' said Mum.

Mum combed Perfect Peter's hair. Then she did it again. And again. And again.

'No nits, Peter,' said Mum, smiling. 'As usual. Well done, darling.'

Perfect Peter smiled modestly.

'It's because I wash and comb my hair every night,' said Peter.

Henry scowled. True, his hair was filthy, but then …

'Nits love clean hair,' said Henry.

'No they don't,' said Peter. '*I've* never ever had nits.'

We'll see about that, thought Henry. When no one was looking he picked a few nits off the paper towel. Then he wandered over to Peter and casually fingered a lock of his hair.

LEAP!

Scratch. Scratch.

'Mum!' squealed Peter. 'Henry's pulling my hair!'

'Stop it, Henry,' said Dad.

'I wasn't pulling his hair,' said Henry indignantly. 'I just wanted to see how clean it was. And it is so lovely and clean,' added Henry sweetly. 'I wish my hair was as clean as Peter's.'

Peter beamed. It wasn't often that Henry said any-thing nice to him.

'Right,' said Mum grimly, 'everyone upstairs. It's shampoo time.'

'NO!' shrieked Horrid Henry.

'NO SHAMPOO!'

He hated the stinky smelly horrible shampoo much more than he hated having nits. Only today his teacher, Miss Battle-Axe, had sent home a nit letter.

BEWARE!
Nits Nits Nits Nits
Nits have been seen
in school
GET RID OF THEM!
Wash your hair with
Supersonic Nit
Blasting Shampoo
PLEASE
OR ELSE.

Naturally, Henry had crumpled up the letter and thrown it away. He was never ever going to have pongy nit shampoo on his head again. What rotten luck Mum had spotted him scratching.

'It's the only way to get rid of nits,' said Dad.

'But it never works!' screamed Henry. And he ran for the door.

Mum and Dad grabbed him. Then they dragged him kicking and screaming to the bathroom.

'Nits are living creatures,' howled Henry. 'Why kill them?'

'Because . . .' said Mum.

'Because . . . because . . . they're blood-sucking nits,' said Dad.

Blood-sucking. Henry had never thought of that. In the split second that he stood still to consider this interesting information, Mum emptied the bottle of supersonic nit-blasting shampoo over his hair.

'NO!' screamed Henry.

Frantically he shook his head. There was shampoo on the door. There was shampoo on the floor. There was shampoo all over Mum and Dad. The only place there was no shampoo was on Henry's head.

'Henry! Stop being horrid!' yelled Dad, wiping shampoo off his shirt.

'What a big fuss over nothing,' said Peter.

Henry lunged at him. Mum seized Henry by the collar and held him back.

'Now Peter,' said Mum. 'That wasn't a kind thing to say to Henry, was it? Not everyone is as brave as you.'

'You're right, Mum,' said Perfect Peter. 'I was being rude and thoughtless. It won't happen again. I'm so sorry, Henry.'

Mum smiled at him. 'That was a perfect apology, Peter. As for you, Henry . . .' she sighed. 'We'll get more shampoo tomorrow.'

Phew, thought Henry, giving his head an extra good scratch. Safe for one more day.

The next morning at school a group of parents burst into the classroom, waving the nit letter and shouting.

'My Margaret doesn't have nits!' shrieked Moody

Margaret's mother. 'She never has and she never will. How dare you send home such a letter!'

'My Josh doesn't have nits,' shouted his mother. 'The idea!'

'My Toby doesn't have nits!' shouted his father. 'Some nasty child in this class isn't bug-busting!'

Miss Battle-Axe squared her shoulders.

'Rest assured that the culprit will be found,' she said. 'I have declared war on nits.'

Scratch. Scratch. Scratch.

Miss Battle-Axe spun round. Her beady eyes swivelled over the class.

'Who's scratching?' she demanded.

Silence.

Henry bent over his worksheet and tried to look studious.

'Henry is,' said Moody Margaret.

'Liar!' shouted Horrid Henry. 'It was William!'

Weepy William burst into tears.

'No it wasn't,' he sobbed.

Miss Battle-Axe glared at the class.

'I'm going to find out once and for all who's got nits,' she growled.

'I don't!' shouted Moody Margaret.

'I don't!' shouted Rude Ralph.

'I don't!' shouted Horrid Henry.

'Silence!' ordered Miss Battle-Axe. 'Nora, the nit nurse, is coming this morning. Who's got nits? Who's not bug-busting? We'll all find out soon.'

Uh-oh, thought Henry. Now I'm sunk. There was no escaping Nitty Nora Bug Explorer and her ferocious combs. Everyone would know *he* had the nits. Rude Ralph would never stop teasing him. He'd be shampooed every night. Mum and Dad would find out about all the nit letters he'd thrown away . . .

He could of course get a tummy ache double quick and be sent home. But Nitty Nora had a horrible way of remembering whose head she hadn't checked and then combing it in front of the whole class.

He could run screaming out of the door saying he'd caught mad cow disease. But somehow he didn't think Miss Battle-Axe would believe him.

There was no way out. This time he was well and truly stuck.

Unless . . .

Suddenly Henry had a wonderful, spectacular idea. It was so wicked, and so horrible, that even Horrid Henry hesitated. But only for a moment. Desperate times call for desperate measures.

Henry leaned over Clever Clare and brushed his head lightly against hers.

LEAP!

Scratch. Scratch.

'Get away from me, Henry,' hissed Clare.

'I was just admiring your lovely picture,' said Henry.

He got up to sharpen his pencil. On his way to the sharpener he brushed against Greedy Graham.

LEAP!

Scratch. Scratch.

On his way back from the sharpener Henry stumbled and fell against Anxious Andrew.

LEAP!

Scratch. Scratch.

'Ow!' yelped Andrew.

'Sorry, Andrew,' said Henry. 'What big clumsy feet I have. Whoops!' he added, tripping over the carpet and banging heads with Weepy William.

LEAP!

Scratch. Scratch.

'Waaaaaaaaa!' wailed William.

'Sit down at once, Henry,' said Miss Battle-Axe. 'William! Stop scratching. Bert! How do you spell cat?'

'I dunno,' said Beefy Bert.

Horrid Henry leaned across the table and put his head close to Bert's.

'C-A-T,' he whispered helpfully.

LEAP!

Scratch. Scratch.

Then Horrid Henry raised his hand.

'Yes?' said Miss Battle-Axe.

'I don't understand these instructions,' said Henry sweetly. 'Could you help me, please?'

Miss Battle-Axe frowned. She liked to keep as far away from Henry as possible. Reluctantly she came closer and bent over his work. Henry leaned his head near hers.

LEAP!

Scratch. Scratch.

There was a pounding at the door. Then Nitty Nora marched into the classroom, bristling with combs and other instruments of torture.

'Line up, everyone,' said Miss Battle-Axe, patting her hair. 'The nit nurse is here.'

Rats, thought Henry. He'd hardly started. Slowly he stood up.

Everyone pushed and shoved to be first in line. Then a few children remembered what they were lining up for and stampeded towards the back. Horrid Henry saw his chance and took it.

He charged through the squabbling children, brushing against everyone as fast as he could.

Scratch! Scratch! LEAP!

LEAP!

Scratch! Scratch!

LEAP!

Scratch! Scratch!

'Henry!' shouted Miss Battle-Axe. 'Stay in at playtime. Now go to the end of the queue. The rest of you, stop this nonsense at once!'

Moody Margaret had fought longest and hardest to be first. Proudly she presented her head to Nitty Nora.

37

'I certainly don't have nits,' she said.

Nitty Nora stuck the comb in.

'Nits!' she announced, stuffing a nit note into Margaret's hand.

For once Margaret was too shocked to speak.

'But . . . but . . .' she gasped.

Tee-hee, thought Henry. Now he wouldn't be the only one.

'Next,' said Nitty Nora.

She stuck the comb in Rude Ralph's greasy hair.

'Nits!' she announced.

'Nit-face,' hissed Horrid Henry, beside himself with glee.

'Nits!' said Nitty Nora, poking her comb into Lazy Linda's mop.

'Nits!' said Nitty Nora, prodding Greedy Graham's frizzy hair.

'Nits, nits, nits, nits, nits!' she continued, pointing at

Weepy William, Clever Clare, Sour Susan, Beefy Bert and Dizzy Dave.

Then Nitty Nora beckoned to Miss Battle-Axe.

'Teachers too,' she ordered.

Miss Battle-Axe's jaw dropped.

'I have been teaching for twenty- five years and I have never had nits,' she said. 'Don't waste your time checking *me*.'

Nitty Nora ignored her protests and stuck in the comb.

'Hmmn,' she said, and whispered in Miss Battle-Axe's ear.

'NO!' howled Miss Battle-Axe. 'NOOOOOOOO!' Then she joined the line of weeping, wailing children clutching their nit notes.

At last it was Henry's turn.

Nitty Nora stuck her comb into Henry's tangled hair

and dragged it along his scalp. She combed again. And again. And again.

'No nits,' said Nitty Nora. 'Keep up the good work, young man.'

'I sure will!' said Henry.

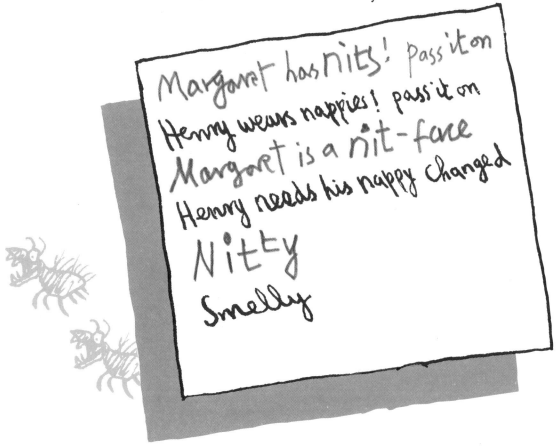

Horrid Henry skipped home waving his certificate.

'Look, Peter,' crowed Henry. 'I'm nit-free!'

Perfect Peter burst into tears.

'I'm not,' he wailed.

'Hard luck,' said Horrid Henry.

Margaret has nits! pass it on
Henry wears nappies! pass it on
Margaret is a nit-face
Henry needs his nappy Changed
Nitty
Smelly

HORRID HENRY'S SCHOOL TRIP

'**D**on't forget my packed lunch for the school trip,' shouted Horrid Henry for the tenth time.

'I want crisps, biscuits, chocolate, and a fizzywizz drink.'

'No way, Henry,' said Dad grimly, slicing carrots. 'I'm making you a healthy, nutritious lunch.'

'But I don't want a healthy lunch,' howled Henry. 'I like sweets!'

'Sweets, yuck,' said Perfect Peter. He peeked in his lunch box.

'Oh boy, an apple!' said Peter. 'And egg and cress on brown bread with the crusts on! And carrot and celery sticks, my favourite! Thank you so much, Dad. Henry, if you don't eat healthy food, you'll never grow big and strong.'

'Oh yeah,' said Henry. 'I'll show you how big and strong I am, you little pipsqueak,' he added, springing at Peter. He was a boa constrictor throttling his prey.

'Uggghhhh,' choked Peter.

'Stop being horrid, Henry!' shouted Mum. 'Or there will be no school trip for you.'

Henry let Peter go. Horrid Henry loved school trips. No work. No assembly. A packed lunch. A chance to fool around all day. What could be better?

'I'm going to the Frosty Freeze Ice Cream factory,' said Henry. 'Free ice creams for everyone. Yippee!'

Perfect Peter made a face. 'I don't like ice cream,' he

said. 'My class is going somewhere much better – our Town Museum. And Mum's coming to help.'

'I'd rather be boiled alive and eaten by cannibals than go to that boring old dump,' said Horrid Henry, shuddering. Mum had dragged him there once. Never again.

Then Henry noticed Peter's T-shirt. It was exactly the same as his, purple striped with gold stars.

'Tell Peter to stop copying what I wear to school!' screamed Henry.

'It doesn't matter, Henry,' said Mum. 'You're going on different trips. No one will notice.'

'Just keep out of my way, Peter,' snarled Henry. 'I don't want anyone to think we're related.'

Horrid Henry's class buzzed with excitement as they scrambled to be first on the bus.

'I've got crisps!' shouted Dizzy Dave.

'I've got biscuits!' shouted Anxious Andrew.

'I've got toffee and chocolate and lollies and three fizzywizzes!' shouted Greedy Graham.

'WAAAA,' wailed Weepy William. 'I forgot my packed lunch.'

'Quiet!' ordered Miss Battle-Axe as the bus started moving. 'Sit still and behave. No eating on the bus. William, stop weeping.'

'I need a wee!' shouted Lazy Linda.

'Well, you'll have to wait,' snapped Miss Battle-Axe.

Horrid Henry had trampled his way to the window seats at the back next to Rude Ralph and Greedy Graham. He liked those seats best. Miss Battle-Axe couldn't see him, and he could make faces at all the people in the cars behind him.

Henry and Ralph rolled down the window and chanted:

'Beans, beans, good for the heart,

The more you eat, the more you –'

'HENRY!' bellowed Miss Battle-Axe. 'Turn around and face forward NOW!'

'I need a wee!' shouted Dizzy Dave.

'Look what I've got, Henry,' said Greedy Graham, holding a bulging bag of sweets.

'Gimme some,' said Henry.

'And me,' said Rude Ralph.

The three boys stuffed their faces with sweets.

'Ugh, a green lime,' said Henry, taking the sticky

sweet out of his mouth. 'Eeech.' He flicked the sweet
away.

PING!

The sweet landed on Moody Margaret's neck.
'Ow,' said Margaret.
She turned round and glared at Henry.
'Stop it, Henry!' she snarled.
'I didn't do anything,' said Henry.

PING!

A sweet landed in Sour Susan's hair.

PING!

A sweet stuck on Anxious Andrew's new jumper.
'Henry's throwing sweets!' shouted Margaret.
Miss Battle-Axe turned round.
'Henry! Sit next to me,' she said.
'I needed a wee!' wailed Weepy William.

Finally, the bus drove up to the Frosty Freeze
Factory. A gigantic, delicious-looking ice cream cone
loomed above it.

'We're here!' shouted Henry.

'You scream! I scream! We all scream for ice cream!' shrieked the children as the bus stopped outside the gate.

'Why are we waiting here?' yelled Greedy Graham. 'I want my ice creams now!'

Henry stuck his head out of the window. The gates were chained shut. A large sign read: 'CLOSED on Mondays.'

Miss Battle-Axe looked pale. 'I don't believe this,' she muttered.

'Class, there's been a mix-up, and we seem to have come on the wrong day,' said Miss Battle-Axe. 'But never mind. We'll go to –'

'The Science Museum!' shouted Clever Clare.

'The zoo!' shouted Dizzy Dave.

'Lazer Zap!' shouted Horrid Henry.

'No,' said Miss Battle-Axe. 'Our Town Museum.'

'Ugggghhhhh,' groaned the class.

No one groaned louder than Horrid Henry.

The children left their jackets and lunch boxes in the packed lunch room, and then followed the museum guide to Room 1.

'First we'll see Mr Jones's collection of rubber bands,' said the guide. 'Then our famous display of door hinges and dog collars through history. And don't worry, you'll be seeing our latest acquisitions, soil from Miss Montague's garden and the Mayor's baby pictures.'

Horrid Henry had to escape.

'I need a wee,' said Henry.

'Hurry up then,' said Miss Battle-Axe. 'And come straight back.'

The toilets were next to the packed lunch room.

Henry thought he'd make sure his lunch was still there. Yup, there it was, right next to Ralph's.

I wonder what Ralph has got, thought Henry, staring at Ralph's packed lunch. No harm in looking.

WOW. Rude Ralph's lunchbox was bursting with crisps, sweets, and a chocolate spread sandwich on white bread.

He'll feel sick if he eats all that junk food, thought Henry. I'd better help him.

It was the work of a moment to swap Ralph's sandwich for Henry's egg and cress.

This certainly isn't very healthy, thought Henry, gazing at Greedy Graham's goodies. I'll do him a favour and exchange a few of my celery sticks for his sweets.

Just look at all those treats, thought Henry, fingering Sour Susan's cakes. She should eat a more balanced meal.

A pack of raisins zipped from Henry's lunchbox to Susan's and a sticky bun leapt from Susan's to Henry's.

Tsk tsk, thought Henry, helping himself to Tough Toby's chocolate bar and replacing it with an apple. Too many sweets are bad for the teeth.

That's better, he thought, gazing at his re-packed lunch with satisfaction. Then he strolled back to his class, who were gathered round a glass case.

'This is the soil in which Miss Montague grew her prize-winning vegetables,' droned the guide. 'She grew marrows, tomatoes, potatoes, leeks –'

'When do we eat?' interrupted Horrid Henry.

'I'm starving,' whined Greedy Graham.

'My tummy's rumbling,' groaned Rude Ralph.

'When's lunch?' moaned Moody Margaret.

'WE'RE HUNGRY!' wailed the children.

'All right,' said Miss Battle-Axe. 'We'll eat now.'

The class stampeded down the hall and grabbed their lunches. Henry sat in a corner and tucked in.

For a moment there was silence, then the room echoed with howls of dismay.

'Where's my sticky bun?' yelped Sour Susan.

'My sweets are gone!' screamed Greedy Graham.

'What's this? Egg and cress? Yuck!' shouted Rude Ralph, hurling the sandwich at Anxious Andrew.

That did it. The room filled with flying carrot and celery sticks, granola bars, raisins, crusts, and apples. Henry smirked as he wiped the last traces of chocolate from his mouth.

'Stop it! Stop it!' howled Miss Battle-Axe. 'Well done, Henry, for being the only sensible child. You may lead us back to see the pieces of Roman pottery in Room 2.'

Horrid Henry walked proudly at the head of the shuffling, whining children. Then he noticed the lift at the far end. A sign read:

STAFF ONLY: DO NOT ENTER

I wonder where that lift goes, thought Horrid Henry.

'Stop him!' yelled a guard.

But it was too late.

Henry had dashed to the lift and pressed the top button.

Up up up he zipped.

Henry found himself in a small room filled with half-finished exhibits. On display were lists of overdue library books, 'lightbulbs from 1965 to today,' and rows and rows of rocks.

Then, in the corner, Henry actually saw something interesting: a dog's skeleton protected by a drooping blue cord.

Henry looked more closely.

It's just a pile of bones, thought Henry.

He wobbled the blue cord then stood on it.

'Look at me, I'm a tightrope walker,' chortled Horrid Henry, swaying on the blue cord. 'I'm the best tight-rope walker in – AGGGHHHH!'

Horrid Henry lost his balance and toppled against the skeleton.

CLITTER-CLATTER! The bones crashed to the ground.

DING DING DING. A burglar alarm began to wail.

Museum guards ran into the room.

Uh-oh, thought Horrid Henry. He slipped between a guard's legs and ran. Behind him he could hear pounding feet.

Henry dashed into a large room filled with road signs, used bus tickets and traffic cones. At the other end of the room Henry saw Peter's class gathered in front of 'The Story of the Drain'. Oh no. There was Mum.

Henry ducked behind the traffic cones.

Museum guards entered.

'There he is!' shouted one. 'The boy in the purple T-shirt with the gold stars.'

Henry stood fixed to the spot. He was trapped. Then the guards ran straight past his hiding place. A long arm reached over and plucked Perfect Peter from his group.

'Come with us, you!' snarled the guard. 'We're going straight to the Bad Children's Room.'

'But . . . but . . .' gasped Peter.

'No ifs or buts!' snapped the guard. 'Who's in charge of this child?'

'I am,' said Mum. 'What's the meaning of this?'

'You come too,' ordered the guard.

'But . . . but . . .' gasped Mum.

Shouting and protesting, Mum and Perfect Peter were taken away.

Then Henry heard a familiar booming voice.

'Margaret, that's enough pushing,' said Miss Battle-Axe. 'No touching, Ralph. Stop weeping, William. Hurry up, everyone! The bus leaves in five minutes. Walk quietly to the exit.'

Everyone immediately started running.

Horrid Henry waited until most of the children had charged past then rejoined the group.

'Where have you been, Henry?' snapped Miss Battle-Axe.

'Just enjoying this brilliant museum,' said Horrid Henry. 'When can we come back?'

HORRID HENRY'S WORST TEACHERS

HORRID HENRY'S
SPORTS DAY

'We all want sports day to be a great success tomorrow,' announced Miss Battle-Axe. 'I am here to make sure that *no one*' – she glared at Horrid Henry – 'spoils it.'

Horrid Henry glared back. Horrid Henry hated sports day. Last year he hadn't won a single event. He'd dropped his egg in the egg-and-spoon race, tripped over Rude Ralph in the three-legged race, and collided with Sour Susan in the sack race. Henry's team had even lost the tug-of-war. Most sickening of all, Perfect Peter had won *both* his races.

If only the school had a sensible day, like TV-watching day, or chocolate-eating day, or who could guzzle the most crisps day, Horrid Henry would be sure to win every prize. But no. *He* had to leap and dash about getting hot and bothered in front of stupid parents. When he became king he'd make teachers run all the races then behead the winners. King Henry the Horrible grinned happily.

'Pay attention, Henry!' barked Miss Battle-Axe. 'What did I just say?'

Henry had no idea. 'Sports day is cancelled?' he suggested hopefully.

Miss Battle-Axe fixed him with her steely eyes. 'I said no one is to bring any sweets tomorrow. You'll all be given a delicious, refreshing piece of orange.'

Henry slumped in his chair, scowling. All he could do was hope for rain.

Sports day dawned bright and sunny. Rats, thought Henry. He could, of course, pretend to be sick. But he'd tried that last year and Mum hadn't been fooled. The year before that he'd complained he'd hurt his leg. Unfortunately Dad then caught him dancing on the table.

It was no use. He'd just have to take part. If only he could win a race!

Perfect Peter bounced into his room.

'Sports day today!' beamed Peter. 'And *I'm* responsible for bringing the hard-boiled eggs for the egg-and-spoon races. Isn't it exciting!'

'NO!' screeched Henry. 'Get out of here!'

'But I only …' began Peter.

Henry leapt at him, roaring. He was a cowboy lassoing a runaway steer.

'Eeeaaargh!' squealed Peter.

'Stop being horrid, Henry!' shouted Dad. '
Or no pocket money this week!'

Henry let Peter go.

'It's so unfair,' he muttered, picking up his clothes from the floor and putting them on. Why did he never win?

Henry reached under his bed and filled his pockets from the secret sweet tin he kept there. Horrid Henry was a master at eating sweets in school without being detected. At least he could scoff something good while the others were stuck eating dried-up old orange pieces.

Then he stomped downstairs. Perfect Peter was busy packing hard-boiled eggs into a carton.

Horrid Henry sat down scowling and gobbled his breakfast.

'Good luck, boys,' said Mum. 'I'll be there to cheer for you.'

'Humph,' growled Henry.

'Thanks, Mum,' said Peter. 'I expect I'll win my egg-and-spoon race again but of course it doesn't matter if I don't. It's *how* you play that counts.'

'Shut up, Peter!' snarled Henry. Egg-and-spoon! Egg-and-spoon! If Henry heard that disgusting phrase once more he would start frothing at the mouth.

'Mum! Henry told me to shut up,' wailed Peter, 'and he attacked me this morning.'

'Stop being horrid, Henry,' said Mum. 'Peter, come with me and we'll comb your hair. I want you to look your best when you win that trophy again.'

Henry's blood boiled. He felt like snatching those eggs and hurling them against the wall.

Then Henry had a wonderful, spectacular idea. It was so wonderful that … Henry heard Mum coming back down the stairs. There was no time to lose crowing about his brilliance.

Horrid Henry ran to the fridge, grabbed another egg carton and swapped it for the box of hard-boiled ones on the counter.

'Don't forget your eggs, Peter,' said Mum. She handed the carton to Peter, who tucked it safely in his school bag.

Tee hee, thought Horrid Henry.

Henry's class lined up on the playing fields. Flash! A small figure wearing gleaming white trainers zipped by. It was Aerobic Al, the fastest boy in Henry's class.

'Gotta run, gotta run, gotta run,' he chanted, gliding into place beside Henry. 'I will, of course, win every event,' he announced. 'I've been training all year. My dad's got a special place all ready for my trophies.'

'Who wants to race anyway?' sneered Horrid Henry, sneaking a yummy gummy fuzzball into his mouth.

'Now, teams for the three-legged race,' barked Miss Battle-Axe into her megaphone. 'This is a race showing how well you cooperate and use teamwork with your partner. Ralph will race with William, Josh will race with Clare, Henry …' she glanced at her list '… you will race with Margaret.'

'NO!' screamed Horrid Henry.

'NO!' screamed Moody Margaret.

'Yes,' said Miss Battle-Axe.

'But I want to be with Susan,' said Margaret.

'No fussing,' said Miss Battle-Axe. 'Bert, where's your partner?'

'I dunno,' said Beefy Bert.

Henry and Margaret stood as far apart as possible while their legs were tied together.

'You'd better do as I say, Henry,' hissed Margaret. '*I'll* decide how we race.'

'*I* will, you mean,' hissed Henry.

'Ready … steady … GO!'

Miss Battle-Axe blew her whistle.

They were off! Henry moved to the left, Margaret moved to the right.

'This way, Henry!' shouted Margaret. She tried to drag him.

'No, this way!' shouted Henry. He tried to drag her.

They lurched wildly, left and right, then toppled over.

CRASH! Aerobic Al and Lazy Linda tripped over the screaming Henry and Margaret.

SMASH! Rude Ralph and Weepy William fell over Al and Linda.

BUMP! Dizzy Dave and Beefy Bert collided with Ralph and William.

'Waaa!' wailed Weepy William.

'It's all your fault, Margaret!' shouted Henry, pulling her hair.

'No, yours,' shouted Margaret, pulling his harder.

Miss Battle-Axe blew her whistle frantically.

'Stop! Stop!' she ordered. 'Henry! Margaret! What an example to set for the younger ones. Any more nonsense like that and you'll be severely punished. Everyone, get ready for the egg-and-spoon race!'

This was it! The moment Henry had been waiting for.

The children lined up in their teams. Moody Margaret, Sour Susan and Anxious Andrew were going

first in Henry's class. Henry glanced at Peter. Yes, there he was, smiling proudly, next to Goody-Goody Gordon, Spotless Sam, and Tidy Ted. The eggs lay still on their spoons. Horrid Henry held his breath.

'Ready … steady … GO!' shouted Miss Battle-Axe.

They were off!

'Go, Peter, go!' shouted Mum.

Peter walked faster and faster and faster. He was in the lead. He was pulling away from the field. Then … wobble … wobble … SPLAT!

'Aaaaagh!' yelped Peter.

Moody Margaret's egg wobbled.

SPLAT!

Then Susan's.

SPLAT!

Then everybody's.

SPLAT!

SPLAT!

SPLAT!

'I've got egg on my shoes!' wailed Margaret.

'I've ruined my new dress!' shrieked Susan.

'I've got egg all over me!' squealed Tidy Ted.

'Help!' squeaked Perfect Peter. Egg dripped down his trousers.

Parents surged forward, screaming and waving hand-kerchiefs and towels.

Rude Ralph and Horrid Henry shrieked with laughter.

Miss Battle-Axe blew her whistle.

'Who brought the eggs?' asked Miss Battle-Axe. Her voice was like ice.

'I did,' said Perfect Peter. 'But I brought hard-boiled ones.'

'OUT!' shouted Miss Battle-Axe. 'Out of the games!'

'But … but …' gasped Perfect Peter.

'No buts, out!' she glared. 'Go straight to the Head.'

Perfect Peter burst into tears and crept away.

Horrid Henry could hardly contain himself. This was the best sports day he'd ever been to.

'The rest of you, stop laughing at once. Parents, get back to your seats! Time for the next race!' ordered Miss Battle-Axe.

All things considered, thought Horrid Henry, lining up with his class, it hadn't been too terrible a day. He'd loved the egg-and-spoon race, of course. And he'd had fun pulling the other team into a muddy puddle in the tug-of-war, knocking over the obstacles in the obstacle race, and crashing into Aerobic Al in the sack race. But, oh, to actually win something!

There was just one race left before sports day was over. The cross-country run. The event Henry hated more than any other. One long, sweaty, exhausting lap round the whole field.

Henry heaved his heavy bones to the starting line. His final chance to win … yet he knew there was no hope. If he beat Weepy William he'd be doing well.

Suddenly Henry had a wonderful, spectacular idea. Why had he never thought of this before? Truly, he was a genius. Wasn't there some ancient Greek who'd won a race by throwing down golden apples which his rival kept stopping to pick up? Couldn't he, Henry, learn something from those old Greeks?

'Ready … steady … GO!' shrieked Miss Battle-Axe. Off they dashed.

'Go, Al, go!' yelled his father.

'Get a move on, Margaret!' shrieked her mother.

'Go, Ralph!' cheered his father.

'Do your best, Henry,' said Mum.

Horrid Henry reached into his pocket and hurled some sweets. They thudded to the ground in front of the runners.

'Look, sweets!' shouted Henry.

Al checked behind him. He was well in the lead. He paused and scooped up one sweet, and then another. He glanced behind again, then started unwrapping the yummy gummy fuzzball.

'Sweets!' yelped Greedy Graham. He stopped to pick up as many as he could find then stuffed them in his mouth.

'Yummy!' screamed Graham.

'Sweets! Where?' chanted the others. Then they stopped to look.

'Over there!' yelled Henry, throwing another handful. The racers paused to pounce on the treats.

While the others munched and crunched, Henry made a frantic dash for the lead.

He was out in front! Henry's legs moved as they had never moved before, pounding round the field. And there was the finishing line!

THUD! THUD! THUD! Henry glanced back. Oh no! Aerobic Al was catching up!

Henry felt in his pocket. He had one giant gob-stopper left. He looked round, panting.

'Go home and take a nap, Henry!' shouted Al, sticking out his tongue as he raced past.

Henry threw down the gob-stopper in front of Al. Aerobic Al hesitated, then skidded to a halt and picked it up. He could beat Henry any day so why not show off a bit?

Suddenly Henry sprinted past. Aerobic Al dashed after him. Harder and harder, faster and faster Henry ran. He was a bird. He was a plane. He flew across the finishing line.

'The winner is … Henry?' squeaked Miss Battle-Axe.

'I've been robbed!' screamed Aerobic Al.

'Hurray!' yelled Henry.

Wow, what a great day, thought Horrid Henry, proudly carrying home his trophy. Al's dad shouting at Miss Battle-Axe and Mum. Miss Battle-Axe and Mum shouting back. Peter sent off in disgrace. And he, Henry, the big winner.

'I can't think how you got those eggs muddled up,' said Mum.

'Me neither,' said Perfect Peter, sniffling.

'Never mind, Peter,' said Henry brightly. 'It's not winning, it's *how* you play that counts.'

HORRID HENRY'S HOMEWORK

Ahhhh, thought Horrid Henry. He turned on the TV and stretched out. School was over. What could be better than lying on the sofa all afternoon, eating crisps and watching TV? Wasn't life grand?

Then Mum came in. She did not look like a mum who thought life was grand. She looked like a mum on the warpath against boys who lay on sofas all afternoon, eating crisps and watching TV.

'Get your feet off the sofa, Henry!' said Mum.

'Unh,' grunted Henry.

'Stop getting crisps everywhere!' snapped Mum.

'Unh,' grunted Henry.

'Have you done your homework, Henry?' said Mum.

Henry didn't answer.

'HENRY!' shouted Mum.

'WHAT!' shouted Henry.

$$22 + 7 = 49 \text{ X}$$

'Have you done your homework?'

'What homework?' said Henry. He kept his eyes glued to the TV.

'Go, Mutants!' he screeched.

'The five spelling words you are meant to learn tonight,' said Mum.

'Oh,' said Henry. 'That homework.'

Horrid Henry hated homework. He had far better things to do with his precious time than learn how to spell 'zipper' or work out the answer to 6 x 7. For weeks

Henry's homework sheets had ended up in the recycling box until Dad found them. Henry swore he had no idea how they got there and blamed Fluffy the cat, but since then Mum and Dad had checked his school bag every day.

Mum snatched the zapper and switched off the telly.

'Hey, I'm watching!' said Henry.

'When are you going to do your homework, Henry?' said Mum.

'SOON!' screamed Henry. He'd just returned from a long, hard day at school. Couldn't he have any peace around here? When he was king anyone who said the word 'homework' would get thrown to the crocodiles.

'I had a phone call today from Miss Battle-Axe,' said Mum. 'She said you got a zero in the last ten spelling tests.'

'That's not *my* fault,' said Henry. 'First I lost the words, then I forgot, then I couldn't read my writing, then I copied the words wrong, then –'

'I don't want to hear any more silly excuses,' said Mum. 'Do you know your spelling words for tomorrow?'

'Yes,' lied Henry.

'Where's the list?' Mum asked.

'I don't know,' said Henry.

'Find it or no TV for a month,' said Mum.

'It's not fair,' muttered Henry, digging the crumpled spelling list out of his pocket.

Mum looked at it.

'There's going to be a test tomorrow,' she said. 'How do you spell "goat"?'

'Don't you know how, Mum?' asked Henry.

'Henry . . .' said Mum.

Henry scowled.

'I'm busy,' moaned Henry. 'I promise I'll tell you right after Mutant Madman. It's my favourite show.'

'How do you spell "goat"?' said Mum.

'G-O-T-E,' snapped Henry.

'Wrong,' said Mum. 'What about "boat"?'

'Why do I have to do this?' wailed Henry.

'Because it's your homework,' said Mum. 'You have to learn how to spell.'

'But why?' said Henry. 'I never write letters.'

'Because,' said Mum. 'Now spell "boat"'.

'B-O-T-T-E,' said Henry.

'No more TV until you do your homework,' said Mum.

'I've done all *my* homework,' said Perfect Peter. 'In fact I enjoyed it so much I've already done tomorrow's homework as well.'

Henry pounced on Peter. He was a cannibal tenderising his victim for the pot.

'Eeeeyowwww!' screamed Peter.

'Henry! Go to your room!' shouted Mum. 'And don't come out until you know *all* your spelling words!'

Horrid Henry stomped upstairs and slammed his bedroom door. This was so unfair! He was far too busy to bother with stupid, boring, useless spelling. For instance, he hadn't read the new Mutant Madman comic book. He hadn't finished drawing that treasure map. And he hadn't even begun to sort his new collection of Twizzle cards. Homework would have to wait.

There was just one problem. Miss Battle-Axe had said that everyone who spelled all their words correctly tomorrow would get a pack of Big Bopper sweets. Henry loved Big Bopper sweets. Mum and Dad hardly ever let him have them. But why on earth did he have to learn spelling words to get some? If he were the teacher, he'd only give sweets to children who couldn't spell. Henry sighed. He'd just have to sit down and learn those stupid words.

4:30. Mum burst into the room. Henry was lying on his bed reading a comic.

'Henry! Why aren't you doing your homework?' said Mum.

'I'll do it in a sec,' said Henry. 'I'm just finishing this page.'

'Henry . . .' said Mum.

Henry put down the comic.

Mum left. Henry picked up the comic.

5.30. Dad burst into the room. Henry was playing with his knights.

'Henry! Why aren't you doing your homework?' said Dad.

'I'm tired!' yawned Henry. 'I'm just taking a little break. It's hard having so much work!'

'Henry, you've only got five words to learn!' said Dad. 'And you've just spent two hours *not* learning them.'

'All right,' snarled Henry. Slowly, he picked up his spelling list. Then he put it down again. He had to get in the mood. Soothing music, that's what he needed. Horrid Henry switched on his cassette player. The terrible sound of the Driller Cannibals boomed through the house.

'OH, I'M A CAN–CAN–CANNIBAL!' screamed Henry, stomping around his room. 'DON'T CALL ME AN ANIMAL JUST 'CAUSE I'M A CAN–CAN–CANNIBAL!'

Mum and Dad stormed into Henry's bedroom and turned off the music.

'That's enough, Henry!' said Dad.

'DO YOUR HOMEWORK!' screamed Mum.

'IF YOU DON'T GET EVERY SINGLE WORD RIGHT IN YOUR TEST TOMORROW THERE WILL BE NO TELEVISION FOR A WEEK!' shouted Dad.

EEEK! No TV *and* no sweets! This was too much. Horrid Henry looked at his spelling words with loathing.

GOAT   BOAT

SAID   STOAT

FRIEND

'I hate goats! I'll never need to spell the word "goat" in my life,' said Henry. He hated goat's cheese. He hated goat's milk. He thought goats were smelly. That was one word he'd definitely never need to know.

The next word was 'boat'. Who needs to spell that, thought Henry. I'm not going to be a sailor when I grow up. I get seasick. In fact, it's bad for my health to learn how to spell 'boat'.

As for 'said', what did it matter if he spelt it 'sed'? It was perfectly understandable, written 'sed.' Only an old fusspot like Miss Battle-Axe would mind such a tiny mistake.

Then there was 'stoat'. What on earth was a stoat? What a mean, sneaky word. Henry wouldn't know a stoat if it sat on him. Of all the useless, horrible words, 'stoat' was the worst. Trust his teacher, Miss Battle-Axe, to make him learn a horrible, useless word like stoat.

The last word was 'friend'. Well, a real friend like Rude Ralph didn't care how the word 'friend' was spelt. As far as Henry was concerned any friend who minded how he spelt 'friend' was no friend. Miss Battle-Axe included that word to torture him.

Five whole spelling words. It was too much. I'll never learn so many words, thought Henry. But what about tomorrow? He'd have to watch Moody Margaret and

Jolly Josh and Clever Clare chomping away at those delicious Big Boppers, while he, Henry, had to gnash his empty teeth. Plus no TV for a week! Henry couldn't live that long without TV! He was sunk. He was doomed to be sweetless, and TV-less.

But wait. What if there was a way to get those sweets without the horrid hassle of learning to spell? Suddenly, Henry had a brilliant, spectacular idea. It was so simple Henry couldn't believe he'd never thought of it before.

He sat next to Clever Clare. Clare always knew the spelling words. All Henry had to do was to take a little peek at her work. If he positioned his chair right, he'd easily be able to see what she wrote. And he wouldn't be copying her, no way. Just double-checking. I am a genius, thought Horrid Henry. 100% right on the test. Loads of Big Bopper sweets. Mum and Dad would be so thrilled they'd let him watch extra TV. Hurray!

Horrid Henry swaggered into class the next morning. He sat down in his seat between Clever Clare and Beefy Bert. Carefully, he inched his chair over a fraction so that he had a good view of Clare's paper.

'Spelling test!' barked Miss Battle-Axe. 'First word – goat.'

Clare bent over her paper. Henry pretended he was staring at the wall, then, quick as a flash, he glanced at her work and wrote 'goat'.

'Boat,' said Miss Battle-Axe. Again Horrid Henry sneaked a look at Clare's paper and copied her. And again. And again.

This is fantastic, thought Henry. I'll never have to learn any spelling words. Just think of all the comic books he could read instead of wasting his time on homework! He sneaked a peek at Beefy Bert's paper. Blank. Ha ha, thought Henry.

There was only one word left. Henry could taste the tingly tang of a Big Bopper already. Wouldn't he swagger about! And no way would he share his sweets with anyone.

Suddenly, Clare shifted position and edged away from him. Rats! Henry couldn't see her paper any more.

'Last word,' boomed Miss Battle-Axe. 'Friend.'

Henry twisted in his seat. He could see the first four words. He just needed to get a tiny bit closer . . .

Clare looked at him. Henry stared at the ceiling. Clare glared, then looked back at her paper. Quickly, Henry leaned over and . . .YES! He copied down the final word, 'friend'.

Victory!

Chomp! Chomp! Chomp! Hmmnn, boy, did those Big Boppers taste great!

Someone tapped him on the shoulder. It was Miss Battle-Axe. She was smiling at him with her great big yellow teeth. Miss Battle-Axe had never smiled at Henry before.

'Well, Henry,' said Miss Battle-Axe. 'What an improvement! I'm thrilled.'

'Thank you,' said Henry modestly.

'In fact, you've done so well I'm promoting you to the top spelling group. Twenty-five extra words a night. Here's the list.'

Horrid Henry's jaws stopped chomping. He looked

in horror at the new spelling list. It was littered with words. But not just any words. Awful words. Mean words. Long words. HARD words.

Hieroglyphs.

Trapezium.

Diarrhoea.

'AAAAAHHHHHHHHHHH!' shrieked Horrid Henry.

Ralph – got any sweets?

No. Graham has

Oye Graham. Give me some sweets

I've already eaten them

Greedy Guts

Poo breath

HORRID HENRY'S SPELLING TEST

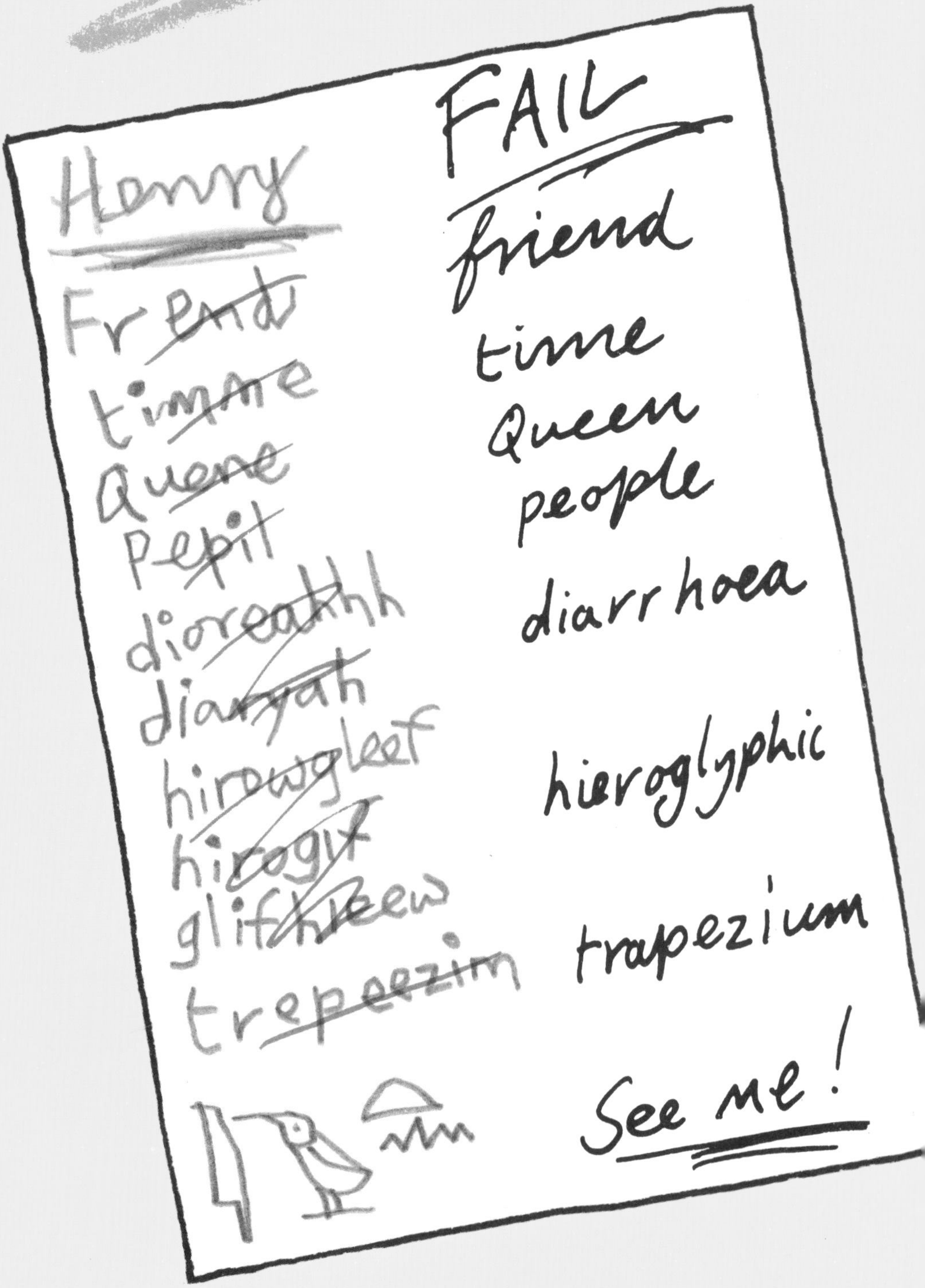

Henry

FAIL

Frend
timne
Quene
Pepit
dioreathh
dianyah
hirowgleef
hirogit
glifhew
trepeezim

friend
time
Queen
people

diarrhoea

hieroglyphic

trapezium

See me!

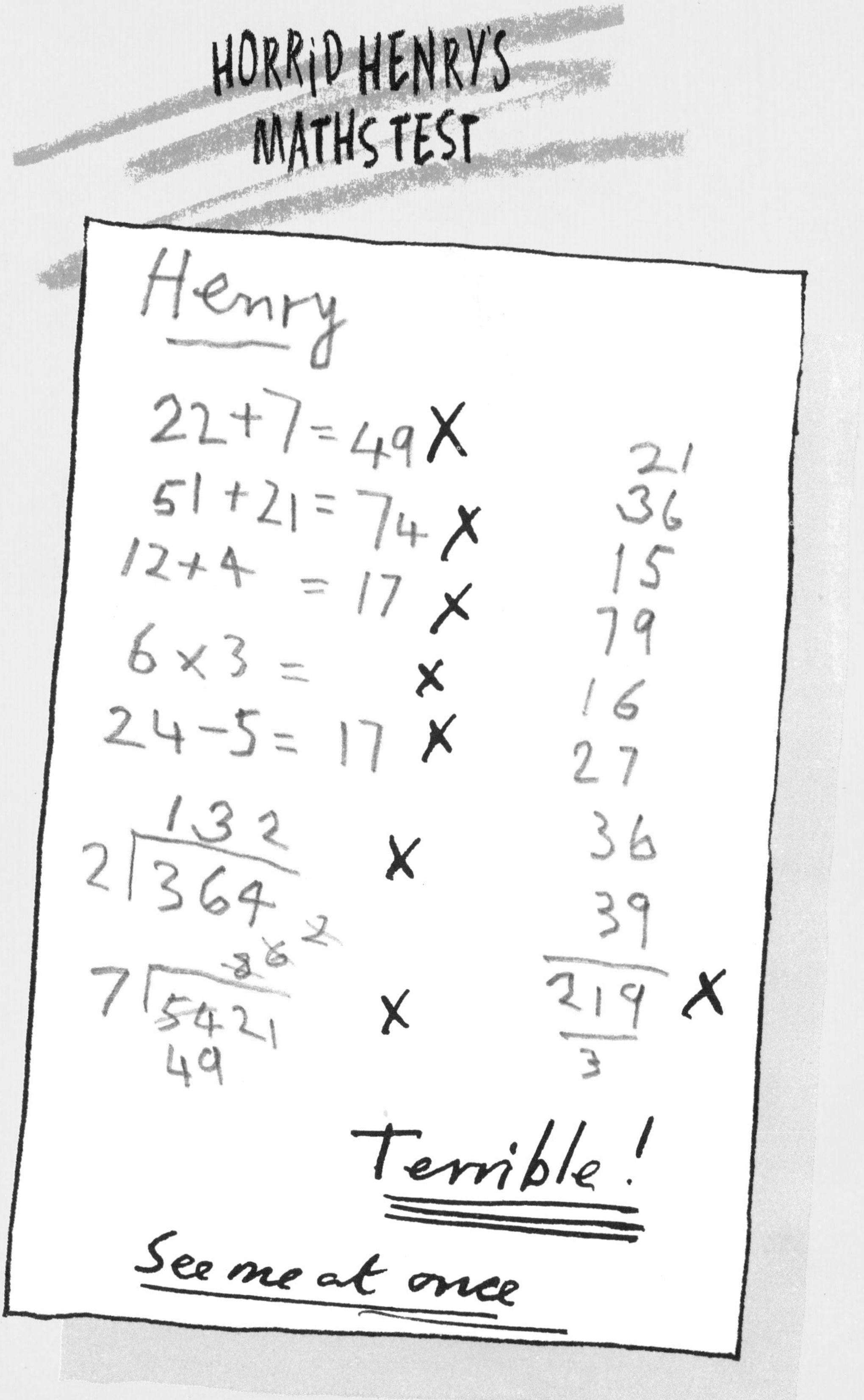

HORRID HENRY'S
MATHS TEST

Henry

$22 + 7 = 49$ ✗

$51 + 21 = 74$ ✗

$12 + 4 = 17$ ✗

$6 \times 3 =$ ✗

$24 - 5 = 17$ ✗

$$2 \overline{)364}^{\,132} \quad ✗$$

$$7 \overline{)5421}^{\,86\,^{2}} \quad ✗$$
$$49$$

21
36
15
79
16
27
36
39
$$\frac{219}{3} \quad ✗$$

Terrible!

See me at once

HORRID HENRY'S SWIMMING LESSON

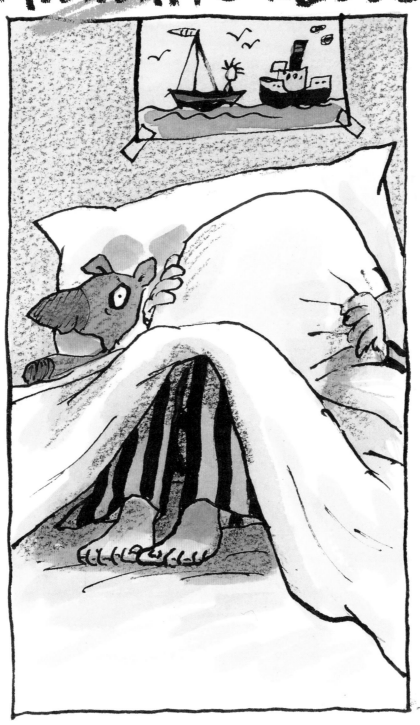

Oh no! thought Horrid Henry. He pulled the duvet tightly over his head. It was Thursday. Horrible, horrible, Thursday. The worst day of the week. Horrid Henry was certain Thursdays came more often than any other day. Thursday was his class swimming day. Henry had a nagging feeling that this Thursday was even worse than all the other awful Thursdays.

Horrid Henry liked the bus ride to the pool. Horrid Henry liked doing the dance of the seven towels in the

changing room. He also liked hiding in the lockers, throwing socks in the pool, and splashing everyone.

The only thing Henry didn't like about going swimming was . . . swimming.

The truth was, Horrid Henry hated water. Ugggh! Water was so . . . wet! And soggy. The chlorine stung his eyes. He never knew what horrors might be lurking in the deep end. And the pool was so cold penguins could fly in for the winter.

Fortunately, Henry had a brilliant list of excuses. He'd pretend he had a verucca, or a tummy ache, or had lost his swimming costume. Unfortunately, the mean, nasty, horrible swimming teacher, Soggy Sid, usually made him get in the pool anyway.

Then Henry would duck Dizzy Dave, or splash Weepy William, or pinch Gorgeous Gurinder, until Sid ordered him out. It was not surprising that Horrid Henry had never managed to get his five-metre badge.

Arrrgh! Now he remembered. Today was test day. The terrible day when everyone had to show how far they could swim. Aerobic Al was going for gold. Moody Margaret was going for silver. The only ones who were still trying for their five-metre badges were Lazy Linda and Horrid Henry. Five whole metres! How could anyone swim such a vast distance?

If only they were tested on who could sink to the

bottom of the pool the fastest, or splash the most, or spit water the furthest, then Horrid Henry would have every badge in a jiffy. But no. He had to leap into a freezing cold pool, and, if he survived that shock, somehow thrash his way across five whole metres without drowning.

Well, there was no way he was going to school today.

Mum came into his room.

'I can't go to school today, Mum,' Henry moaned. 'I feel terrible.'

Mum didn't even look at him.

'Thursday-itis again, I presume,' said Mum.

'No way!' said Henry. 'I didn't even know it was Thursday.'

'Get up Henry,' said Mum. 'You're going swimming and that's that.'

Perfect Peter peeked round the door.

'It's badge day today!' he said. 'I'm going for 50 metres!'

'That's brilliant, Peter,' said Mum. 'I bet you're the best swimmer in your class.'

Perfect Peter smiled modestly.

'I just try my best,' he said. 'Good luck with your five-metre badge, Henry,' he added.

Horrid Henry growled and attacked. He was a Venus flytrap slowly mashing a frantic fly between his deadly leaves.

'Eeeeeowwww!' screeched Peter.

'Stop being horrid, Henry!' screamed Mum. 'Leave your poor brother alone!'

Horrid Henry let Peter go. If only he could find some way not to take his swimming test he'd be the happiest boy in the world.

Henry's class arrived at the pool. Right, thought Henry. Time to unpack his excuses to Soggy Sid.

'I can't go swimming, I've got a verucca,' lied Henry.

'Take off your sock,' ordered Soggy Sid.

Rats, thought Henry.

'Maybe it's better now,' said Henry.

'I thought so,' said Sid.

Horrid Henry grabbed his stomach.

'Tummy pains!' he moaned. 'I feel terrible.'

'You seemed fine when you were prancing round the pool a moment ago,' snapped Sid. 'Now get changed.'

Time for the killer excuse.

'I forgot my swimming costume!' said Henry. This was his best chance of success.

'No problem,' said Soggy Sid. He handed Henry a bag. 'Put on one of these.'

Slowly, Horrid Henry rummaged in the bag. He pulled out a bikini top, a blue costume with a hole in the middle, a pair of pink pants, a tiny pair of green trunks, a polka-dot one piece with bunnies, see-through white shorts, and a nappy.

'I can't wear any of these!' protested Horrid Henry.

'You can and you will, if I have to put them on you myself,' snarled Sid.

Horrid Henry squeezed into the green trunks. He could barely breathe. Slowly, he joined the rest of his class pushing and shoving by the side of the pool.

Everyone had millions of badges sewn all over their

costumes. You couldn't even see Aerobic Al's bathing suit beneath the stack of badges.

'Hey you!' shouted Soggy Sid. He pointed at Weepy William. 'Where's your swimming costume?'

Weepy William glanced down and burst into tears.

'Waaaaah,' he wailed, and ran weeping back to the changing room.

'Now get in!' ordered Soggy Sid.

'But I'll drown!' screamed Henry. 'I can't swim!'

'Get in!' screamed Soggy Sid.

Goodbye, cruel world. Horrid Henry held his breath and fell into the icy water. ARRRRGH! He was turning into an iceberg!

He was dying! He was dead! His feet flailed madly as he sank down, down, down – clunk! Henry's feet touched the bottom.

Henry stood up, choking and spluttering. He was waist-deep in water.

'Linda and Henry! Swim five metres – now!'

What am I going to do? thought Henry. It was so humiliating not even being able to swim five metres! Everyone would tease him. And he'd have to listen to them bragging about their badges! Wouldn't it be great to get a badge? Somehow?

Lazy Linda set off, very very slowly. Horrid Henry grabbed on to her leg. Maybe she'll pull me across, he thought.

'Ugggh!' gurgled Lazy Linda.

'Leave her alone!' shouted Sid. 'Last chance, Henry.'

Horrid Henry ran along the pool's bottom and flapped his arms, pretending to swim.

'Did it!' said Henry.

Soggy Sid scowled.

'I said swim, not walk!' screamed Sid. 'You've failed. Now get over to the far lane and practise. Remember, anyone who stops swimming during the test doesn't get a badge.'

Horrid Henry stomped over to the far lane. No way was he going to practise! How he hated swimming! He watched the others splashing up and down, up and down. There was Aerobic Al, doing his laps like a bolt of

lightning. And Moody Margaret. And Kung-Fu Kate. Everyone would be getting a badge but Henry. It was so unfair.

'Pssst, Susan,' said Henry. 'Have you heard? There's a shark in the deep end!'

'Oh yeah, right,' said Sour Susan. She looked at the dark water in the far end of the pool.

'Don't believe me,' said Henry. 'Find out the hard way. Come back with a leg missing.'

Sour Susan paused and whispered something to Moody Margaret.

'Shut up, Henry,' said Margaret. They swam off.

'Don't worry about the shark, Andrew,' said Henry. 'I think he's already eaten today.'

'What shark?' said Anxious Andrew.

Andrew stared at the deep end. It did look awfully dark down there.

'Start swimming, Andrew!' shouted Soggy Sid.

'I don't want to,' said Andrew.

'Swim! Or I'll bite you myself!' snarled Sid.

Andrew started swimming.

'Dave, Ralph, Clare, and Bert – start swimming!' bellowed Soggy Sid.

'Look out for the shark!' said Horrid Henry. He watched Aerobic Al tearing up and down the lane. 'Gotta swim, gotta swim, gotta swim,' muttered Al between strokes.

What a show-off, thought Henry. Wouldn't it be fun to play a trick on him?

Horrid Henry pretended he was a crocodile. He sneaked under the water to the middle of the pool and waited until Aerobic Al swam overhead. Then Horrid Henry reached up.

Pinch! Henry grabbed Al's thrashing leg.

'AAAARGGG!' screamed Al. 'Something's grabbed my leg. Help!' Aerobic Al leaped out of the pool.

Tee hee, thought Horrid Henry.

'It's a shark!' screamed Sour Susan. She scrambled out of the pool.

'There's a shark in the pool!' screeched Anxious Andrew.

'There's a shark in the pool!' howled Rude Ralph.

Everyone was screaming and shouting and struggling to get out.

The only one left in the pool was Henry.

Shark!

Horrid Henry forgot there were no sharks in swimming pools.

Horrid Henry forgot he'd started the shark rumour.

Horrid Henry forgot he couldn't swim.

All he knew was that he was alone in the pool – with a shark!

Horrid Henry swam for his life. Shaking and quaking, splashing and crashing, he torpedoed his way to the side of the pool and scrambled out. He gasped and panted. Thank goodness. Safe at last! He'd never ever go swimming again.

'Five metres!' bellowed Soggy Sid. 'You've all failed your badges today, except for – Henry!'

'Waaaaaaahhhhhh!' wailed the other children.

'Whoopee!' screamed Henry. 'Olympics, here I come!'

HORRID HENRY
AND THE
DEMON DINNER LADY

'**Y**ou're not having a packed lunch and that's final,' yelled Dad.

'It's not fair!' yelled Horrid Henry. 'Everyone in my class has a packed lunch.'

'N–O spells no,' said Dad. 'It's too much work. And you never eat what I pack for you.'

'But I hate school dinners!' screamed Henry. 'I'm being poisoned!' He clutched his throat. 'Dessert today was – bleeeach – fruit salad! And it had worms in it! I can feel them slithering in my stomach – uggghh!' Horrid Henry fell to the floor, gasping and rasping.

Mum continued watching TV.

Dad continued watching TV.

'I love school dinners,' said Perfect Peter. 'They're so nutritious and delicious. Especially those lovely spinach salads.'

'Shut up, Peter!' snarled Henry.

'Muuuum!' wailed Peter. 'Henry told me to shut up!'

'Don't be horrid, Henry!' said Mum. 'You're not having a packed lunch and that's that.'

Horrid Henry and his parents had been fighting about packed lunches for weeks. Henry was desperate to have a packed lunch. Actually, he was desperate not to have a school dinner.

Horrid Henry hated school dinners. The stinky smell. The terrible way Sloppy Sally ladled the food *splat*! on his tray so that most of it splashed all over him. And the food! Queueing for hours for revolting ravioli and squashed tomatoes. The lumpy custard. The blobby mashed potatoes. Horrid Henry could not bear it any longer.

'Oh please,' said Henry. 'I'll make the packed lunch myself.' Wouldn't that be great! He'd fill his lunchbox with four packs of crisps, chocolate, doughnuts, cake, lollies, and one grape. Now that's what I call a real lunch, thought Henry.

Mum sighed.

Dad sighed.

They looked at each other.

'If you promise that everything in your lunchbox will get eaten, then I'll do a packed lunch for you,' said Dad.

'Oh thank you thank you thank you!' said Horrid Henry. 'Everything will get eaten, I promise.' Just not by me, he thought gleefully. Packed lunch room, here I come. Food fights, food swaps, food fun at last. Yippee!

Horrid Henry strolled into the packed lunch room. He was King Henry the Horrible, surveying his unruly subjects. All around him children were screaming and

shouting, pushing and shoving, throwing food and trading treats. Heaven! Horrid Henry smiled happily and opened his Terminator Gladiator lunchbox.

Hmmn. An egg salad sandwich. On brown bread. With crusts. Yuck! But he could always swap it for one of Greedy Graham's stack of chocolate spread sandwiches. Or one of Rude Ralph's jam rolls. That was the great thing about packed lunches, thought Henry. Someone always wanted what you had. No one *ever* wanted someone else's school dinner. Henry shuddered.

But those bad days were behind him, part of the dim and distant past. A horror story to tell his grandchildren. Henry could see it now. A row of horrified toddlers, screaming and crying while he told terrifying tales of stringy stew and soggy semolina.

Now, what else? Henry's fingers closed on something round. An apple. Great, thought Henry, he could use it for target practice, and the carrots would be perfect for poking Gorgeous Gurinder when she wasn't looking.

Henry dug deeper. What was buried right at the

bottom? What was hidden under the celery sticks and the granola bar? Oh boy! Crisps! Henry loved crisps. So salty! So crunchy! So yummy! His mean, horrible parents only let him have crisps once a week. Crisps! What bliss! He could taste their delicious saltiness already. He wouldn't share them with anyone, no matter how hard they begged. Henry tore open the bag and reached in –

Suddenly a huge shadow fell over him. A fat greasy hand shot out. Snatch! Crunch. Crunch.

Horrid Henry's crisps were gone.

Henry was so shocked that for a moment he could not speak. 'Wha–wha–what was that?' gasped Henry as a gigantic woman waddled between the tables. 'She just stole my crisps!'

'That,' said Rude Ralph grimly, 'was Greta. She's the demon dinner lady.'

'Watch out for her!' squealed Sour Susan.

'She's the sneakiest snatcher in school,' wailed Weepy William.

What? A dinner lady who snatched food instead of dumping it on your plate? How could this be? Henry stared as Greasy Greta patrolled up and down the aisles. Her piggy eyes darted from side to side. She ignored Aerobic Al's carrots. She ignored Tidy Ted's yoghurt.

She ignored Goody-Goody Gordon's
orange.

Then suddenly –

Snatch! Chomp. Chomp. Sour Susan's
sweets were gone.

Snatch! Chomp.
Chomp. Dizzy Dave's
doughnut was gone.
Snatch! Chomp.
Chomp. Beefy Bert's
biscuits were gone.
Moody Margaret
looked up from her lunch.
'Don't look up!'
shrieked Susan. Too late! Greasy Greta swept
Margaret's food away, stuffing Margaret's uneaten
chocolate bar into her fat wobbly cheeks.

'Hey, I wasn't finished!' screamed Margaret. Greasy
Greta ignored her and marched on. Weepy William
tried to hide his toffees under his cheese sandwich. But
Greasy Greta wasn't fooled.

Snatch! Gobble. Gobble. The toffees vanished down
Greta's gaping gob.

'Waaah,' wailed William. 'I want my toffees!'

'No sweets in school,' barked Greasy Greta. She
marched up and down, up and down, snatching and
grabbing, looting and devouring, wobbling and gobbling.

Why had no one told him there was a demon dinner
lady in charge of the packed lunch room?

'Why didn't you warn me about her, Ralph?'
demanded Henry.

Rude Ralph shrugged. 'It wouldn't have done any
good. She is unstoppable.'

We'll see about that, thought Henry. He glared at
Greta. No way would Greasy Greta grab his food again.

On Tuesday Greta snatched Henry's doughnut.

On Wednesday Greta snatched Henry's cake.

On Thursday Greta snatched Henry's biscuits.

On Friday, as usual, Horrid Henry persuaded Anxious Andrew to swap his crisps for Henry's granola bar. He persuaded Kung-Fu Kate to swap her chocolates for Henry's raisins. He persuaded Beefy Bert to swap his biscuits for Henry's carrots. But what was the use of being a brilliant food trader, thought Henry miserably, if Greasy Greta just swooped and snaffled his hard-won treats?

Henry tried hiding his desserts. He tried eating his desserts secretly. He tried tugging them back. But it was no use. The moment he snapped open his lunchbox – SNATCH! Greasy Greta grabbed the goodies.

Something had to be done.

'Mum,' complained Henry, 'there's a demon dinner lady at school snatching our sweets.'

'That's nice, Henry,' said Mum, reading her newspaper.

'Dad,' complained Henry, 'there's a demon dinner lady at school snatching our sweets.'

'Good,' said Dad. 'You eat too many sweets.'

'We're not allowed to bring sweets to school, Henry,' said Perfect Peter.

'But it's not fair!' squealed Henry. 'She takes crisps, too.'

'If you don't like it, go back to school dinners,' said Dad.

'No!' howled Henry. 'I hate school dinners!' Watery gravy with bits. Lumpy surprise with lumps. Gristly glop with globules. Food with its own life slopping

about on his tray. NO! Horrid Henry couldn't face it. He'd fought so hard for a packed lunch. Even a packed lunch like the one Dad made, fortified with eight essential minerals and vitamins, was better than going back to school dinners.

He could, of course, just eat healthy foods. Greta
never snatched those. Henry imagined his lunchbox,
groaning with alfalfa sprouts on wholemeal brown
bread studded with chewy bits. Ugh! Bleeeach!
Torture!

He had to keep his packed lunch. But he had to stop
Greta. He just had to.

And then suddenly Henry had a brilliant, spectacular
idea. It was so brilliant that for a moment he could
hardly believe he'd thought of it. Oh boy, Greta,
thought Henry gleefully, are you going to be sorry you
messed with me.

Lunchtime. Horrid Henry sat with his lunchbox
unopened. Rude Ralph was armed and ready beside
him. Now, where was Greta?

Thump. Thump. Thump. The floor shook as the
demon dinner lady started her food patrol. Horrid
Henry waited until she was almost behind him. SNAP!

He opened his lunchbox.

SNATCH! The familiar greasy hand shot out, grabbed Henry's biscuits and shovelled them into her mouth. Her terrible teeth began to chomp.

And then –

'Yiaowwww! Aaaarrrgh!' A terrible scream echoed through the packed lunch room.

Greasy Greta turned purple. Then pink. Then bright red.

'Yiaowwwww!' she howled. 'I need to cool down! Gimme that!' she screeched, snatching Rude Ralph's doughnut and stuffing it in her mouth.

'Aaaarrrgh!' she choked. 'I'm on fire! Water! Water!'

She grabbed a pitcher of water, poured it on top of herself, then ran howling down the aisle and out the door.

For a moment there was silence. Then the entire packed lunch room started clapping and cheering.

'Wow, Henry,' said Greedy Graham, 'what did you do to her?'

'Nothing,' said Horrid Henry. 'She just tried my special recipe. Hot chilli powder biscuits, anyone?'

HORRID HENRY
READS A BOOK

Blah blah blah blah blah.

Miss Battle-Axe droned on and on and on.

Horrid Henry drew pictures of crocodiles tucking into a juicy Battle-Axe snack in his maths book.

Snap! Off went her head.

Yank! Bye bye leg.

Crunch! Ta-ta teeth.

Yum yum. Henry's crocodile had a big fat smile on its face.

Blah blah blah books blah blah blah read blah blah blah prize blah blah

. . . PRIZE?

Horrid Henry stopped doodling.

'What prize?' he shrieked.

'Don't shout out, Henry,' said Miss Battle-Axe.

Horrid Henry waved his hand and shouted:

'What prize?'

'Well, Henry, if you'd been paying attention instead of scribbling, you'd know, wouldn't you?' said Miss Battle-Axe.

Horrid Henry scowled. Typical teacher. You're interested enough in what they're saying to ask a question, and suddenly they don't want to answer.

'So class, as I was saying before I was so rudely interrupted –' she glared at Horrid Henry – 'you'll have two weeks to read as many books as you can for our school reading competition. Whoever reads the most books will win an exciting prize. A very exciting prize. But remember, a book report on every book on your list, please.'

Oh. A reading competition. Horrid Henry slumped in his chair. Phooey. Reading was hard, heavy work. Just turning the pages made Henry feel exhausted. Why couldn't they ever do fun competitions, like whose tummy could rumble the loudest, or who shouted out the most in class, or who knew the rudest words? Horrid Henry would win *those* competitions every time.

But no. Miss Battle-Axe would never have a *fun* competition. Well, no way was he taking part in a reading contest. Henry would just have to watch some-one undeserving like Clever Clare or Brainy Brian swagger off with the prize while he sat prize-less at the back. It was so unfair!

'What's the prize?' shouted Moody Margaret.

Probably something awful like a pencil case, thought Horrid Henry. Or a bumper pack of school tea towels.

'Sweets!' shouted Greedy Graham.

'A million pounds!' shouted Rude Ralph.

'Clothes!' shouted Gorgeous Gurinder.

'A skateboard!' shouted Aerobic Al.

'A hamster!' said Anxious Andrew.

'Silence!' bellowed Miss Battle-Axe. 'The prize is a family ticket to a brand new theme park.'

Horrid Henry sat up. A theme park! Oh wow! He loved theme parks! Rollercoasters! Water rides! Candy floss! His mean, horrible parents never took him to theme parks. They dragged him to museums. They hauled him on hikes. But if he won the competition, they'd have to take him. He had to win that prize. He had to. But how could he win a reading competition without reading any books?

'Do comics count?' shouted Rude Ralph.

Horrid Henry's heart leapt. He was king of the comic book readers. He'd easily win a comic book competition.

Miss Battle-Axe glared at Ralph with her beady eyes.

'Of course not!' she said. 'Clare! How many books do you think you can read?'

'Fifteen,' said Clever Clare.

'Brian?'

'Eighteen,' said Brainy Brian.

'Nineteen,' said Clare.

'Twenty,' said Brian.

Horrid Henry smiled. Wouldn't they get a shock when he won the prize? He'd start reading the second he got home.

Horrid Henry stretched out in the comfy black chair

and switched on the TV. He had plenty of time to read. He'd start tomorrow.

Tuesday. Oh boy! Five new comics! He'd read them first and start on all those books later.

Wednesday. Whoopee! A Mutant Max TV special! He'd definitely get reading afterwards.

Thursday. Rude Ralph brought round his great new computer game, 'Mash 'em! Smash 'em!' Henry mashed and smashed and mashed and smashed . . .

Friday. Yawn. Horrid Henry was exhausted after his long, hard week. I'll read tons of books tomorrow, thought Henry. After all, there was loads of time till the competition ended.

'How many books have you read, Henry?' asked Perfect Peter, looking up from the sofa.

'Loads,' lied Henry.

'I've read five,' said Perfect Peter proudly. 'More than anyone in my class.'

'Goody for you,' said Henry.

'You're just jealous,' said Peter.

'As if I'd ever be jealous of you, worm,' sneered Henry. He wandered over to the sofa. 'So what are you reading?'

'*The Happy Nappy*,' said Peter.

The Happy Nappy! Trust Peter to read a stupid book like that.

'What's it about?' asked Henry, snorting.

'It's great,' said Peter. 'It's all about this nappy –' Then he stopped. 'Wait, I'm not telling *you*. You just want to find out so you can use it in the competition. Well, you're too late. Tomorrow is the last day.'

Horrid Henry felt as if a dagger had been plunged into his heart. This couldn't be. Tomorrow! How had tomorrow sneaked up so fast?

'What!' shrieked Henry. 'The competition ends – tomorrow?'

'Yes,' said Peter. 'You should have started reading sooner. After all, why put off till tomorrow what you can do today?'

'Shut up!' said Horrid Henry. He looked around wildly. What to do, what to do. He had to read something, anything – fast.

'Gimme that!' snarled Henry, snatching Peter's book. Frantically, he started to read:

'I'm unhappy, pappy,' said the snappy nappy. 'A happy nappy is a clappy –'

Perfect Peter snatched back his book.

'No!' screamed Peter, holding on tightly. 'It's mine.'

Henry lunged.

'Mine!'

'Mine!'

Riii—iippp.

'MUUUUMMMM!' screamed Peter. 'Henry tore my book!'

Mum and Dad ran into the room.

'You're fighting—over a book?' said Mum. She sat down in a chair.

'I'm speechless,' said Mum.

'Well, I'm not,' said Dad. 'Henry! Go to your room!'

'Fine!' screamed Horrid Henry.

Horrid Henry prowled up and down his bedroom. He had to think of something. Fast.

Aha! The room was full of books. He'd just copy down lots of titles. Phew. Easy-peasy.

And then suddenly Horrid Henry remembered. He had to write a book report for every book he read. Rats. Miss Battle-Axe knew loads and loads of books. She was sure to know the plot of *Jack the Kangaroo* or *The Adventures of Terry the Tea Towel*.

Well, he'd just have to borrow Peter's list.

Horrid Henry sneaked into Peter's bedroom. There was Peter's competition entry, in the centre of Peter's immaculate desk. Henry read it.

Of course Peter would have the boring and horrible *Mouse Goes to Town*. Could he live with the shame of having baby books like *The Happy Nappy* and *Mouse Goes to Town* on his competition entry?

For a day at a theme park, anything.

Quickly, Henry copied Peter's list and book reports. Whoopee! Now he had five books. Wheel of Death here I come, thought Horrid Henry.

Then Henry had to face the terrible truth. Peter's books wouldn't be enough to win. He'd heard Clever Clare had seventeen. If only he didn't have to write those book reports. Why oh why did Miss Battle-Axe have to know every book ever written?

And then suddenly Henry had a brilliant, spectacular idea. It was so brilliant, and so simple, that Horrid Henry was amazed. Of course there were books that Miss Battle-Axe didn't know. Books that hadn't been written – yet.

Horrid Henry grabbed his list.

'*Mouse Goes to Town*. The thrilling adventures of a mouse in town. He meets a dog, a cat, and a duck.'

Why should that poor mouse just go to town? Quickly Henry began to scribble.

'*Mouse Goes to the Country.* The thrilling adventures of a mouse in the country. He meets –'

Henry paused. What sort of things did you meet in the country? Henry had no idea.

Aha. Henry wrote quickly. 'He meets a sheep and a werewolf.'

'*Mouse Goes Round the World.* Mouse discovers that the world is round.'

'*Mouse Goes to the Loo.* The thrilling adventures of one mouse and his potty.'

Now, perhaps, something a little different. How about *A Boy and his Pig.* What could that book be about? thought Henry.

'Once upon a time there was a boy and his pig. They played together every day. The pig went oink.'

Sounds good to me, thought Henry.

Then there was *A Pig and his Boy*. And, of course, *A Boyish Pig. A Piggish Boy. Two Pigs and a Boy. Two Boys and a Pig.*

Horrid Henry wrote and wrote and wrote. When he had filled up four pages with books and reports, and his hand ached from writing, he stopped and counted.

Twenty-seven books! Surely that was more than enough!

Miss Battle-Axe rose from her seat and walked to the podium in the school hall. Horrid Henry was so excited he could scarcely breathe. He had to win. He was sure to win.

'Well done, everyone,' said Miss Battle-Axe. 'So many wonderful books read. But sadly, there can be only one winner.'

Me! thought Horrid Henry.

'The winner of the school reading competition, the winner who will be receiving a fabulous prize, is –' Horrid Henry got ready to leap up – 'Clare, with twenty-eight books!'

Horrid Henry sank back down in his seat as Clever Clare swaggered up to the podium. If only he'd added *Three Boys, Two Pigs, and a Rhinoceros* to his list, he'd have tied for first. It was so unfair. All his hard work for nothing.

'Well done, Clare!' beamed Miss Battle-Axe. She waved Clare's list. 'I see you've read one of my very favourites, *Boudicca's Big Battle.*'

She stopped. 'Oh dear. Clare, you've put down *Boudicca's Big Battle* twice by mistake. But never mind. I'm sure no one else has read *twenty-seven* books –'

'I have!' screamed Horrid Henry. Leaping and shouting, punching the air with his fist,

124

Horrid Henry ran up onto the stage, chanting: 'Theme park! Theme park! Theme park!'

'Gimme my prize!' he screeched, snatching the tickets out of Clare's hand.

'Mine!' screamed Clare, snatching them back.

Miss Battle-Axe looked grim. She scanned Henry's list.

'I am not familiar with the *Boy and Pig* series,' she said.

'That's 'cause it's Australian,' said Horrid Henry.

Miss Battle-Axe glared at him. Then she tried to twist her face into a smile.

'It appears we have a tie,' she said. 'Therefore, you will each receive a family pass to the new theme park, Book World. Congratulations.'

Horrid Henry stopped his victory dance. Book World? Book World? Surely he'd heard wrong?

'Here are just some of the wonderful attractions you will enjoy at Book World,' said Miss Battle-Axe. ' 'Thrill to a display of speed-reading! Practice checking out library books! Read to the beat! Oh my, doesn't that sound fun!'

'AAAAAARGGGGGGGGG!' screamed Horrid Henry.

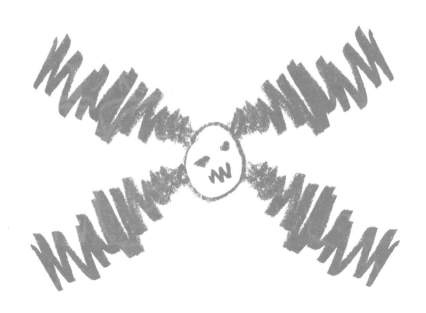

HORRID HENRY'S
SCHOOL PROJECT

'**S**usan! Stop shouting!

Ralph! Stop running!

William! Stop weeping!

Henry! Just stop!'

Miss Battle-Axe glared at her class. Her class glared back.

'Miss!' screeched Lazy Linda. 'Henry's pulling my hair.'

'Miss!' screeched Gorgeous Gurinder. 'Ralph's kicking me.'

'Miss!' screeched Anxious Andrew. 'Dave's poking me.'

'Stop it, Henry!' barked Miss Battle-Axe.

Henry stopped. What was bothering the old bat now?

'Class, pay attention,' said Miss Battle-Axe. 'Today we're doing Group Projects on the Ancient Greeks. We're studying –'

'– the sacking of Troy!' shrieked Henry. Yes! He could see it now. Henry, leading the Greeks as they crashed and slashed their way through the terrified Trojans. His spear would be the longest, and the sharpest, and –

Miss Battle-Axe fixed Henry with her icy stare. Henry froze.

'We're going to divide into small groups and make Parthenons out of cardboard loo rolls and card,' continued Miss Battle-Axe. 'First you must draw the Parthenon, agree a design together, then build and paint it. I want to see *everyone* sharing and listening. Also, the Head Teacher will be dropping by to admire your work and to see how beautifully you are working together.'

Horrid Henry scowled. He hated working in groups. He detested sharing. He loathed listening to others. Their ideas were always wrong. His ideas were always right. But the other children in Henry's groups never recognised Henry's genius. For some reason they wanted to do things *their* way, not his.

The Ancient Greeks certainly never worked together beautifully, thought Horrid Henry resentfully, so why should he? They just speared each other or ate their children for tea.

'Henry, Bert, William, and Clare, you're working together on Table Three,' said Miss Battle-Axe.

Horrid Henry groaned. What a horrible, horrible group. He hated all of them. Why did Miss Battle-Axe never put him in a fun group, with Ralph or Graham or Dave? Henry could see it now. They'd be laughing together in the corner, making trumpets out of loo rolls, sneaking sweets, throwing crayons, flicking paint, having a great time.

But oh no. He had to be with bossyboots Clare, crybaby William and – Bert. Miss Battle-Axe did it on purpose, just to torture him.

'NO!' protested Horrid Henry. 'I can't work with *her*!'

'NO!' protested Clever Clare. 'I can't work with *him*!'

'Waaaaah,' wailed Weepy William. 'I want to work with Andrew.'

'Silence!' shouted Miss Battle-Axe. 'Now get in your groups and get to work. I want to see everyone sharing and working together beautifully – or else.'

There was a mad scramble as everyone ran to their tables to grab the best pencils and the most pieces of paper.

Henry snatched the purple, blue and red pencils and a big pile of paper.

'I haven't got any paper!' screamed William.

'Tough,' said Horrid Henry. 'I need all these for my design.'

'I want some paper!' whined William.

Clever Clare passed him one of her sheets.

William burst into tears.

'It's dirty,' he wailed. 'And I haven't got a pencil.'

'Here's what we're going to do,' said Henry. 'I'm doing the design, William can help me build it, and everyone can watch me paint.'

'No way, Henry,' said Clare. 'We *all* do a design, then we make the best one.'

'Which will be mine,' said Horrid Henry.

'Doubt it,' said Clever Clare.

'Well I'm not making *yours*,' snarled Henry. 'And *I'm* doing the painting.'

'You're doing the glueing, *I'm* doing the painting,' said Clare.

'I want to do the painting,' wailed William.

'What do you want to do, Bert?' asked Clare.

'I dunno,' said Beefy Bert.

'Fine,' said Clever Clare. 'Bert will do the tidying. Let's get drawing, everyone. We want our group's Parthenon to be the best.'

Horrid Henry was outraged.

'Who made you boss?' demanded Henry.

'Someone has to take charge,' said Clever Clare.

Horrid Henry reached under the table and kicked her.

'OOWWWW!' yelped Clever Clare. 'Miss! Henry kicked me!'

'Did not!' shouted Horrid Henry. 'Liar.'

'Why isn't Table Three drawing?' hissed Miss Battle-Axe.

Clare drew.

William drew.

Bert drew.

Henry drew.

'Everyone should have finished drawing by now,' said Miss Battle-Axe, patrolling among the tables. 'Time to combine your ideas.'

'But I haven't finished,' wept William.

Horrid Henry gazed at his design with satisfaction. It was a triumph. He could see it now, painted silver and purple, with a few red stripes.

'Why don't we just build mine?' said Clare.

''Cos mine's the best!' shouted Horrid Henry.

'What about mine?' whispered William.

'We're building mine!' shouted Clare.

'MINE!'

'MINE!'

Miss Battle-Axe ran over.

'Stop shouting!' shouted Miss Battle-Axe. 'Show me your work. That's lovely, Clare. What a fabulous design.'

'Thank you, miss,' said Clever Clare.

'William! That's a tower, not a temple! Start again!'

'Waaaah!' wailed William.

'Bert! What is this mess?'

'I dunno,' said Beefy Bert.

'It looks like a teepee, not a temple,' said Miss Battle-Axe.

She looked at Horrid Henry's design and glared at him.

'Can't you follow instructions?' she shrieked. 'That temple looks like it's about to blast off.'

'That's how I meant it to look,' said Henry. 'It's high-tech.'

'Margaret! Sit down! Toby! Leave Brian alone! Graham! Get back to work,' said Miss Battle-Axe, racing off to stop the fight on Table Two.

'Right, we're doing *my* design,' said Clare. 'Who wants to build the steps and who wants to decorate the columns?'

'No one,' snapped Horrid Henry, ''cos we're doing *mine*.'

'Fine, we'll vote,' said Clare. 'Who wants to build mine?'

Clare and William raised their hands.

'I'll get you for that, William,' muttered Henry.

William burst into tears.

'Who wants to do Henry's?' said Clare.

Only Henry raised his hand.

'Come on Bert, don't you want to make mine?' pleaded Henry.

'I dunno,' said Beefy Bert.

'It's not fair!' shrieked Horrid Henry. 'I WANT TO BUILD MINE!'

'MINE!'

'MINE!'

'SLAP!'

'SLAP!

'That's it!' shrieked Miss Battle-Axe. 'Henry! Work in the corner on your own.'

YES! This was the best news Henry had heard all morning.

Beaming, Henry went to the corner and sat down at his own little table, with his own glue, his own scissors, his own paints, his own card, and his own pile of loo rolls.

Bliss, thought Henry. I can build my Parthenon in peace.

There was just one problem. There was only a small number of loo rolls left.

This isn't nearly enough for my Parthenon, thought Horrid Henry. I need more.

He went over to Moody Margaret's table.

'I need more loo rolls,' he said.

'Tough,' said Margaret, 'we're using all of ours.'

Henry stomped over to Sour Susan's table.

'Give me some loo rolls,' he said.

'Go away,' said Susan sourly. 'Margaret took our extras.'

'Sit down, Henry,' barked Miss Battle-Axe.

Henry sat, fuming. This was an outrage. Hadn't Miss Battle-Axe told them to share? And here were his greedy classmates hogging all the loo rolls when his Parthenon desperately needed extra engines.

BUZZZ. Breaktime!

'Leave your Parthenons on the tables to dry,' said Miss Battle-Axe. 'Henry, you will stay in at break and finish.'

What?

Miss break?

'But – but –'

'Sit down,' ordered Miss Battle-Axe. 'Or you'll go straight to the Head!'

Eeeek! Horrid Henry knew the Head, Mrs Oddbod, all too well. He did not need to know her any better.

Henry slunk back to his chair. Everyone else ran shrieking out of the door to the playground. Why was it always children who were punished? Why weren't teachers ever sent to the Head? It was so unfair!

'I just have to nip down the hall for a moment. Don't you dare leave that table,' said Miss Battle-Axe.

The moment Miss Battle-Axe left the room, Henry jumped up and accidentally on purpose knocked over Clare's chair. He broke William's pencil and drew a skull and crossbones on Bert's teepee.

Then he wandered over to Sour Susan's table. There was a freshly-glued Parthenon, waiting to be painted.

Henry studied it.

You know, he thought, Susan's group hasn't done a bad job. Not bad at all. Shame about that bulge on the side, though. If they shared one loo roll with me, it would balance so much better.

Horrid Henry looked to the left.

He looked to the right.

Snatch! Susan's supports sagged.

Better even that up, thought Horrid Henry.

Yank!

Hmmn, thought Horrid Henry, glancing at Gurinder's table. What were they thinking?

Those walls are far too tall.

Grab! Gurinder's temple tottered.

And as for Clare's pathetic efforts, it was positively bursting with useless pillars.

Whisk! Clare's columns wobbled.

Much better, thought Horrid Henry. Soon he had plenty of loo rolls.

CLOMP

CLOMP

CLOMP

Horrid Henry dashed back to his table and was innocently glueing away as the class stampeded back to their tables.

Wobble

Wobble

Wobble – CRASH!

On every table, Parthenons started collapsing.

Everyone shrieked and screamed and sobbed.

'It's your fault!'

'Yours!'

'You didn't glue it right!'

'You didn't build it right!'

Rude Ralph hurled a paintbrush at Moody Margaret. Margaret hurled it back. Suddenly the room was filled with flying brushes, gluepots and loo rolls.

Miss Battle-Axe burst in.

'STOP IT!' bellowed Miss Battle-Axe, as a loo roll hit her on the nose. 'YOU ARE THE WORST CLASS I HAVE EVER TAUGHT! I LEAVE YOU ALONE FOR ONE MINUTE AND JUST LOOK AT THIS MESS! NOW SIT DOWN AND SHUT –'

The door opened. In walked the Head.

Mrs Oddbod stared at Miss Battle-Axe.

Miss Battle-Axe stared at Mrs Oddbod.

'Boudicca!' said Mrs Oddbod. 'What-is-going-on?'

'The sacking of Troy!' shrieked Horrid Henry.

There was a terrible silence.

Horrid Henry shrank in his seat. Now he was done for. Now he was dead.

'I can see that,' said Mrs Oddbod coldly. 'Miss Battle-Axe! Come to my office – now!'

'No!' whimpered Miss Battle-Axe.

YES! thought Horrid Henry.

Victory!

HORRID HENRY'S DOODLES

Ralph, did you see
Terminator Gladiator
last night?
Yeah!
Bet I could be on that show
No way Henry
Course I could
Nah
Just watch me

HORRID HENRY'S UNDERPANTS

A late birthday present! Whoopee! Just when you thought you'd got all your loot, more treasure arrives.

Horrid Henry shook the small thin package. It was light. Very light. Maybe it was – oh, please let it be – MONEY! Of course it was money. What else could it be? There was so much stuff he needed: a Mutant Max lunchbox, a Rapper Zapper Blaster, and, of course, the new Terminator Gladiator game he kept seeing advertised on TV. Mum and Dad were so mean and horrible, they wouldn't buy it for him. But he could buy whatever he liked with his own money. So there. Ha ha ha ha ha. Wouldn't Ralph be green with envy when he swaggered into school with a Mutant Max lunchbox? And no way would he even let Peter touch his Rapper Zapper Blaster.

So how much money had he been sent? Maybe enough for him to buy everything! Horrid Henry tore off the wrapping paper.

AAAAARRRRGGGHHHHH! Great-Aunt Greta had done it again.

Great-Aunt Greta thought he was a girl. Great-Aunt Greta had been told ten billion times that his name was Henry, not Henrietta, and that he wasn't four years old. But every year Peter would get £10, or a football, or a computer game, and he would get a Walkie-Talkie-Teasy-Weasy-Burpy-Slurpy Doll. Or a Princess

Pamper Parlour. Or Baby Poopie Pants. And now this.

Horrid Henry picked up the birthday card. Maybe there was money inside. He opened it.

Dear Henny,
You must be such a big girl now, so I know you'd love a pair of big girl pants. I'll bet pink is your favourite colour.
Love, Great-Aunt Greta

Horrid Henry stared in horror at the frilly pink lacy knickers, decorated with glittery hearts and bows. This was the worst present he had ever received. Worse than socks. Worse than handkerchiefs. Even worse than a book.

Bleeech! Ick! Yuck! Horrid Henry chucked the hideous underpants in the bin where they belonged.

Ding dong.

Oh no! Rude Ralph was here to play. If he saw those knickers Henry would never hear the end of it. His name would be mud forever.

Clump clump clump.

Ralph was stomping up the stairs to his bedroom. Henry snatched the terrible pants from the bin and

looked around his room wildly for a hiding place.
Under the pillow? What if they had a pillow fight?
Under the bed? What if they played hide and seek?
Quickly Henry stuffed them in the back of his pants
drawer. I'll get rid of them the moment Ralph leaves,
he thought.

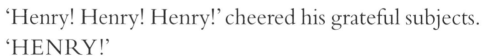

'Mercy, Your Majesty,
mercy!'

King Henry the
Horrible looked down
at his snivelling brother.

'Off with his head!' he
ordered.

'Henry! Henry! Henry!' cheered his grateful subjects.
'HENRY!'

King Henry the Horrible woke up. His Medusa
mother was looming above him.

'You've overslept!' shrieked Mum. 'School starts in
five minutes! Get dressed! Quick! Quick!' She pulled
the duvet off Henry.

'Wha–wha?' mumbled Henry.

Dad raced into the room.

'Hurry!' shouted Dad. 'We're late!' He yanked Henry
out of bed.

Henry stumbled around his dark bedroom. Half-asleep, he reached inside his underwear drawer, grabbed a pair, then picked up some clothes off the floor and flung everything on. Then he, Dad, and Peter ran all the way to school.

'Margaret! Stop pulling Susan's hair!'

'Ralph! Sit down!'

'Linda! Sit up!'

'Henry! Pay attention!' barked Miss Battle-Axe. 'I am about to explain long division. I will only explain it once. You take a great big number, like 374, and then divide it – '

Horrid Henry was not paying attention. He was tired. He was crabby. And for some reason his pants were itchy.

These pants feel horrible, he thought. And so tight. What's wrong with them?

Horrid Henry
sneaked a peek.

And then Horrid
Henry saw what
pants he had on. Not
his Driller Cannibal
pants. Not his
Marvin the Maniac
ones either. Not
even his old Gross-Out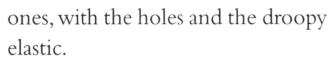
ones, with the holes and the droopy
elastic.

He, Horrid Henry, was wearing frilly pink lacy
girls' pants covered in glittery hearts and bows. He'd
completely forgotten he'd stuffed them into his pants
drawer last month so Ralph wouldn't see them. And
now, oh horror of horrors, he was wearing them.

Maybe it's a nightmare, thought Horrid Henry
hopefully. He pinched his arm. Ouch! Then, just to be
sure, he pinched William.

'Waaaaah!' wailed Weepy William.

'Stop weeping, William!' said Miss Battle-Axe. 'Now,
what number do I need –'

It was not a nightmare. He was still in school, still
wearing pink pants.

What to do, what to do?

Don't panic, thought Horrid Henry. He took a deep

breath. Don't panic. After all, no one will know. His trousers weren't see-through or anything.

Wait. What trousers was he wearing? Were there any holes in them? Quickly Horrid Henry twisted round to check his bottom.

Phew. There were no holes. What luck he hadn't put on his old jeans with the big rip but a new pair.

He was safe.

'Henry! What's the answer?' said Miss Battle-Axe.

'Pants,' said Horrid Henry before he could stop himself.

The class burst out laughing.

'Pants!' screeched Rude Ralph.

'Pants!' screeched Dizzy Dave.

'Henry. Stand up,' ordered Miss Battle-Axe.

Henry stood. His heart was pounding.

Slip!

Aaaarrrghhh! The lacy ruffle of his pink pants was showing! His new trousers were too big. Mum always bought him clothes that were way too big so he'd grow into them. These were the falling-down ones he'd tried on yesterday. Henry gripped his trousers tight and yanked them up.

'What did you say?' said Miss Battle-Axe slowly.

'Ants,' said Horrid Henry.

'Ants?' said Miss Battle-Axe.

'Yeah,' said Henry quickly. 'I was just thinking about how many ants you could divide by – by that number you said,' he added.

Miss Battle-Axe glared at him.

'I've got my eye on you, Henry,' she snapped. 'Now sit down and pay attention.'

Henry sat. All he had to do was tuck in his T-shirt. That would keep his trousers up. He'd look stupid but for once Henry didn't care.

Just so long as no one ever knew about his pink lacy pants.

And then Henry's blood turned to ice. What was the latest craze on the playground? De-bagging. Who'd started it? Horrid Henry. Yesterday he'd chased Dizzy Dave and pulled down his trousers.

The day before he'd done the same thing to Rude Ralph. Just this morning he'd de-bagged Tough Toby on the way into class.

They'd all be trying to de-bag him now.

I have to get another pair of pants, thought Henry desperately.

Miss Battle-Axe passed round the maths worksheets. Quickly Horrid Henry scribbled down: 3, 7, 41, 174, without reading any questions. He didn't have time for long division.

Where could he find some other pants? He could pretend to be sick and get sent home from school. But he'd already tried that twice this week. Wait. Wait. He was brilliant. He was a genius. What about the Lost and Found? Someone, some time, must have lost some pants.

$6 \times 3 =$

DING! DING!

Before the playtime bell had finished ringing Horrid Henry was out of his seat and racing down the hall, holding tight to his trousers. He checked carefully to make sure no one was watching, then ducked into the Lost and Found. He'd hide here until he found some pants.

The Lost and Found was stuffed with clothes. He rummaged through the mountains of lost shoes, socks, jackets, trousers, shirts, coats, lunchboxes, hats, and gloves. I'm amazed anyone leaves school wearing

anything, thought Horrid Henry, tossing another sweat-shirt over his shoulder.

Then – hurray! Pants. A pair of blue pants. What a wonderful sight.

Horrid Henry pulled the pants from the pile. Oh no. They were the teeniest, tiniest pair he'd ever seen. Some toddler must have lost them.

Rats, thought Horrid Henry. Well, no way was he wearing his horrible pink pants a second longer. He'd just have to trade pants with someone. And Horrid Henry had the perfect someone in mind.

Henry found Peter in the playground playing tag with Tidy Ted.

'I need to talk to you in private,' said Henry. 'It's urgent.'

'What about?' said Peter cautiously.

'It's top secret,' said Henry. Out of the corner of his eye he saw Dave and Toby sneaking towards him.

Top secret! Henry never shared top secret secrets with Peter.

'Quick!' yelped Henry. 'There's no time to lose!'

He ducked into the boys' toilet. Peter followed.

'Peter, I'm worried about you,' said Horrid Henry. He tried to look concerned.

'I'm fine,' said Peter.

'No you're not,' said Henry. 'I've heard bad things about you.'

'What bad things?' said Peter anxiously. Not – not that he had run across the carpet in class?

'Embarrassing rumours,' said Horrid Henry. 'But if I don't tell you, who will? After all,' he said, putting his arm around Peter's shoulder, 'it's my job to look after you. Big brothers should look out for little ones.'

Perfect Peter could not believe his ears.

'Oh, Henry,' said Peter. 'I've always wanted a brother who looked after me.'

'That's me,' said Henry. 'Now listen. I've heard you wear baby pants.'

'I do not,' said Peter. 'Look!'

And he showed Henry his Daffy and her Dancing Daisies pants.

Horrid Henry's heart went cold. Daffy and her Dancing Daisies! Ugh. Yuck. Gross. But even Daffy would be a million billion times better than pink pants with lace ruffles.

'Daffy Daisy are the most babyish pants you could wear,' said Henry. 'Worse than wearing a nappy. Everyone will tease you.'

Peter's lip trembled. He hated being teased.

'What can I do?' he asked.

Henry pretended to think. 'Look. I'll do you a big favour. I'll swap my pants for yours. That way *I'll* get teased, not you.'

'Thank you, Henry,' said Peter. 'You're the best brother in the world.' Then he stopped.

'Wait a minute,' he said suspiciously, 'let's see your pants.'

'Why?' said Henry.

'Because,' said Peter, 'how do I know you've even got pants to swap?'

Horrid Henry was outraged.

'Of course I've got pants,' said Henry.

'Then show me,' said Peter.

Horrid Henry was trapped.

'OK,' he said, giving Peter a quick flash of pink lace.

Perfect Peter stared at Henry's underpants.

'Those are your pants?' he said.

'Sure,' said Horrid Henry. 'These are big boy pants.'

'But they're pink,' said Peter.

'All big boys wear pink,' said Henry.

'But they have lace on them,' said Peter.

'All big boys' pants have lace,' said Henry.

'But they have hearts and bows,' said Peter.

'Of course they do, they're big boy pants,' said Horrid Henry. 'You wouldn't know because you only wear baby pants.'

Peter hesitated.

'But . . . but . . . they look like – girls' pants,' said Peter.

Henry snorted. 'Girls' pants! Do you think *I'd* ever wear girls' pants? These are what all the big kids are wearing. You'll be the coolest kid in class in these.'

Perfect Peter backed away.

'No I won't,' said Peter.

'Yes you will,' said Henry.

'I don't want to wear your smelly pants,' said Peter.

'They're not smelly,' said Henry. 'They're brand new. Now give me your pants.'

'NO!' screamed Peter.

'YES!' screamed Henry. 'Give me your pants!'

'What's going on in here?' came a voice of steel. It was the Head, Mrs Oddbod.

'Nothing,' said Henry.

'There's no hanging about the toilets at playtime,' said Mrs Oddbod. 'Out of here, both of you.'

Peter ran out the door.

Now what do I do, thought Horrid Henry.

Henry ducked into a stall and hid the pink pants on the ledge above the third toilet. No way was he putting those pants back on. Better Henry no pants than Henry pink pants.

At lunchtime Horrid Henry dodged Graham. He dodged Toby by the climbing frame. During last play Dave almost caught him by the water fountain but Henry was too quick. Ralph chased him into class but Henry got to his seat just in time. He'd done it! Only forty-five minutes to go until home time. There'd be no de-bagging after school with parents around. Henry couldn't believe it. He was safe at last.

He stuck out his tongue at Ralph.

'Nah nah ne nah ne,' he jeered.

Miss Battle-Axe clapped her claws.

'Time to change for P.E.,' said Miss Battle-Axe.

P.E! It couldn't be – not a P.E. day.

'And I don't care if aliens stole your P.E. kit, Henry,' said Miss Battle-Axe, glaring at him. 'No excuses.'

That's what she thought. He had the perfect excuse. Even a teacher as mean and horrible as Miss Battle-Axe would not force a boy to do P.E. without pants.

Horrid Henry went up to Miss Battle-Axe and whispered in her ear.

'Forgot your pants, eh?' barked Miss Battle-Axe loudly.

Henry blushed scarlet. When he was king he'd make Miss Battle-Axe walk around town every day wearing pants on her head.

'Well, Henry, today is your lucky day,' said Miss Battle-Axe, pulling something pink and lacy out of her pocket. 'I found these in the boys' toilets.'

'Take them away!' screamed Horrid Henry.

HORRID HENRY'S

Best friend
Rude Ralph

Worst enemy
Moody Margaret

Worst school dinner
Lumpy surprise with lumps

Best school dinner
Chips with chips

Worst subjects
Spelling
Maths
P.E.
History
Etc.

Favourite Subject
Lunch

Best Book
The Mummy's Curse

Worst Book
The Happy Nappy

Best Poem
'I'm Gonna Throw Up'

Most boring school trip
Our town museum

Prizes
Trophy for winning the cross-country
run on Sports Day
Family ticket to Book World for winning
the reading competition

Badge
5 metre swimming badge

Best day at school
Getting rid of Mr Nerdon

Worst days at school
Being moved to the top spelling group
Wearing girls' pants

Happiest moment
Sending Miss Battle-Axe to the Head

Scariest moments
Injections
Nitty Nora's inspection

Worst time of the week
Monday, 8.00 am

Best time of the week
Friday, 3.30 pm

Bert   susan   Violet   Kate   Jim   Josh

Henry   Andrew   Brian   Gurinder   Dave   Ralph   Ba

HORRID HENRY'S CLASS

Toby Zoe Nick Fiona Bob Soraya

Graham Margaret William Clare Linda Al

Grandma   Dad   Mum

Fluffy

Henry   Peter   Steve

Great-Aunt Greta

Aunt Ruby

HORRID HENRY'S FAMILY

Fang

Vera

Paul

Polly

Henry

HORRID HENRY
AND THE
COMFY BLACK CHAIR

Ah, Saturday! Best day of the week, thought Horrid Henry, flinging off the covers and leaping out of bed. No school! No homework! A day of TV heaven! Mum and Dad liked sleeping in on a Saturday. So long as Henry and Peter were quiet they could watch TV until Mum and Dad woke up.

Horrid Henry could picture it now. He would stretch out in the comfy black chair, grab the remote control, and switch on the TV. All his favourite shows were on today: *Rapper Zapper, Mutant Max*, and *Gross-Out*. If he hurried he would be just in time for *Rapper Zapper*.

He thudded down the stairs and flung open the sitting room door. A horrible sight met his eyes.

There, stretched out on the comfy black chair and clutching the remote control, was his younger brother, Perfect Peter.

Henry gasped. How could this be? Henry always got downstairs first. The TV was already on. But it was not switched to *Rapper Zapper*. A terrible tinkly tune trickled out of the TV. Oh no! It was the world's most boring show, *Daffy and her Dancing Daisies*.

'Switch the channel!' ordered Henry. '*Rapper Zapper*'s on.'

'That's a horrid, nasty programme,' said Perfect Peter, shuddering. He held tight to the remote.

'I said switch the channel!' hissed Henry.

'I won't!' said Peter. 'You know the rules. The first one downstairs gets to sit in the comfy black chair and decides what to watch. And I want to watch *Daffy*.'

Henry could hardly believe his ears. Perfect Peter was ... refusing to obey an order?

'NO!' screamed Henry. 'I hate that show. I want to watch *Rapper Zapper*!'

'Well, I want to watch *Daffy*,' said Perfect Peter.

'But that's a baby show,' said Henry.

'Dance, my daisies, dance!' squealed the revolting Daffy.

'La, la la la la!' trilled the daisies.

'La, la la la la!' sang Peter.

'Baby, baby!' taunted Henry. If only he could get Peter to run upstairs crying then *he* could get the chair.

'Peter is a baby, Peter is a baby!' jeered Henry.

Peter kept his eyes glued to the screen.

Horrid Henry could stand it no longer. He pounced on Peter, snatched the remote, and pushed Peter onto the floor. He was Rapper Zapper liquidizing a pesky android.

'AAAAAH!' screamed Perfect Peter. 'MUUUMMM!'

Horrid Henry leaped into the comfy black chair and switched channels.

'Grrrrrrr!' growled Rapper Zapper, blasting a baddie.

'DON'T BE HORRID, HENRY!' shouted Mum, storming through the door. 'GO TO YOUR ROOM!'

'NOOOO!' wailed Henry. 'Peter started it!'

'NOW!' screamed Mum.

'La, la la la la!' trilled the daisies.

BUZZZZZZZZ.

Horrid Henry switched off the alarm. It was six a.m. the following Saturday. Henry was taking no chances. Even if he had to grit his teeth and watch *Rise and Shine* before *Gross-Out* started it was worth it. And he'd seen the coming attractions for today's *Gross-Out*: who could eat the most cherry pie in five minutes while blasting the other contestants with a goo-shooter. Henry couldn't wait.

There was no sound from Peter's room. Ha, ha, thought Henry. He'll have to sit on the lumpy sofa and watch what *I* want to watch.

Horrid Henry skipped into the sitting room. And stopped.

'Remember, children, always eat with a knife and fork!' beamed a cheerful presenter. It was *Manners with Maggie*. There was Perfect Peter in his slippers and dressing gown, stretched out on the comfy black chair. Horrid Henry felt sick. Another Saturday ruined! He had to watch *Gross-Out*! He just had to.

Horrid Henry was just about to push Peter off the chair when he stopped. Suddenly he had a brilliant idea.

'Peter! Mum and Dad want to see you. They said it's urgent!'

Perfect Peter leaped off the comfy black chair and dashed upstairs.

Tee hee, thought Horrid Henry.

ZAP!

'Welcome to *GROSS-OUT*!' shrieked the presenter, Marvin the Maniac. 'Boy, will you all be feeling sick today! It's GROSS! GROSS! GROSS!'

'Yeah!' said Horrid Henry. This was great!

Perfect Peter reappeared.

'They didn't want me,' said Peter. 'And they're cross because I woke them up.'

'They told me they did,' said Henry, eyes glued to the screen.

Peter stood still.

'Please give me the chair back, Henry.'

Henry didn't answer.

'I had it first,' said Peter.

'Shut up, I'm trying to watch,' said Henry.

'Ewwwwww, gross!' screamed the TV audience.

'I was watching *Manners with Maggie*,' said Peter. 'She's showing how to eat soup without slurping.'

'Tough,' said Henry. 'Oh, gross!' he chortled, pointing at the screen.

Peter hid his eyes.

'Muuuuummmmmmmmm!' shouted Peter. 'Henry's being mean to me!'

Mum appeared in the doorway.

She looked furious.

'Henry, go to your room!' shouted Mum. 'We were trying to sleep. Is it too much to ask to be left in peace one morning a week?'

'But Peter –'

Mum pointed to the door.

'Out!' said Mum.

'It's not fair!' howled Henry, stomping off.

ZAP!

'And now Kate, our guest manners expert, will demonstrate the proper way to butter toast.'

Henry slammed the door behind him as hard as he could. Peter had got the comfy black chair for the very last time.

BUZZZZZZZ.

Horrid Henry switched off the alarm. It was two a.m. the *following* Saturday. The *Gross-Out* Championships were on in the morning. He grabbed his pillow and duvet and sneaked out of the room. He was taking no chances. Tonight he would *sleep* in the comfy black chair. After all, Mum and Dad had never said how *early* he could get up.

Henry tiptoed out of his room into the hall.

All quiet in Peter's room.

All quiet in Mum and Dad's.

Henry crept down the stairs and carefully opened the sitting room door. The room was pitch black. Better not turn on the light, thought Henry. He felt his way along the wall until his fingers touched the back of the comfy black chair. He felt around the top. Ah, there was the remote. He'd sleep with that under his pillow, just to be safe.

Henry flung himself onto the chair and landed on something lumpy.

'AHHHHHHHHH!' screamed Henry.

'AHHHHHHHHH!' screamed the Lump.

'HELP!' screamed Henry and the Lump.

Feet pounded down the stairs.

'What's going on down there?' shouted Dad, switching on the light.

Henry blinked.

'Henry jumped on my head!' snivelled a familiar voice beneath him.

'Henry, what are you doing?' said Dad. 'It's two o'clock in the morning!'

Henry's brain whirled. 'I thought I heard a burglar so I crept down to keep watch.'

'Henry's lying!' said Peter, sitting up. 'He came down because he wanted the comfy black chair.'

'Liar!' said Henry. 'And what were *you* doing down here?'

'I couldn't sleep and I didn't want to wake you, Dad,' said Peter. 'So I came down as quietly as I could to get a drink of water. Then I felt sleepy and lay down for a moment. I'm very sorry, Dad, it will never happen again.'

'All right,' said Dad, stifling a yawn. 'From now on, you are not to come down here before seven a.m. or there will be no TV for a week! Is that clear?'

'Yes, Dad,' said Peter.

'Yeah,' muttered Henry.

He glared at Perfect Peter.

Perfect Peter glared at Horrid Henry. Then they both went upstairs to their bedrooms and closed the doors.

'Goodnight!' called Henry cheerfully. 'My, I'm sleepy.'

But Henry did not go to bed. He needed to think.

He *could* wait until everyone was asleep and sneak back down. But what if he got caught? No TV for a week would be unbearable.

But what if he missed the *Gross-Out* Championships? And never found out if Tank Thomas or Tapioca Tina won the day? Henry shuddered. There had to be a better way.

Ahh! He had it! He would set his clock ahead and make sure he was first down. Brilliant! *Gross-Out* here I come, he thought.

But wait. What if Peter had the *same* brilliant idea? That would spoil everything. Henry had to double-check.

Henry opened his bedroom door. The coast was clear. He tiptoed out and sneaked into Peter's room.

There was Peter, sound asleep. And there was his clock. Peter hadn't changed the time. Phew.

And then Henry had a truly wicked idea. It was so evil, and so horrid, that for a moment even he hesitated. But hadn't Peter been horrible and selfish, stopping Henry watching his favourite shows? He certainly had. And wouldn't it be great if Peter got into trouble, just for once?

Perfect Peter rolled over. 'La, la la la la,' he warbled in his sleep.

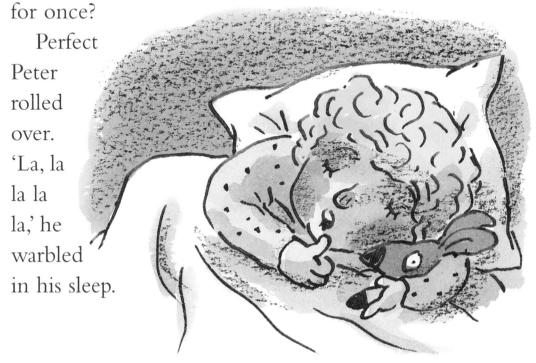

That did it. Horrid Henry moved Peter's clock an hour ahead. Then Henry sneaked downstairs and turned up the TV's volume as loud as it would go.

Finally, he opened Mum and Dad's door, and crept back to bed.

'IT'S GROW AND SHOW! THE VEGETABLE SHOW FOR TINIES! JUST LOOK AT ALL THESE LOVELY VEGETABLES!'

The terrible noise boomed through the house, blasting Henry out of bed.

'HENRY!' bellowed Dad. 'Come here this instant!'

Henry sauntered into his parents' bedroom.

'What is it?' he asked, yawning loudly.

Mum and Dad looked confused.

'Wasn't that you watching TV downstairs?'

'No,' said Henry, stretching. 'I was asleep.'

Mum looked at Dad.

Dad looked at Mum.

'You mean *Peter* is downstairs watching TV at six a.m.?'

Henry shrugged.

'Send Peter up here this minute!' said Dad.

For once Henry did not need to be asked twice. He ran downstairs and burst into the sitting room.

'I grew carrots!'

'I grew string beans!'

'Peter! Mum and Dad want to see you right away!' said Henry.

Peter didn't look away from *Grow and Show*.

'PETER! Dad asked me to send you up!'

'You're just trying to trick me,' said Peter.

'You'd better go or you'll be in big trouble,' said Henry.

'Fool me once, shame on you. Fool me twice, shame on me,' said Peter. 'I'm not moving.'

'Now, just look at all these beautiful tomatoes Timmy's grown,' squealed the TV.

'Wow,' said Peter.

'Don't say I didn't warn you,' said Henry.

'PETER!' bellowed Dad. 'NO TV FOR A
MONTH! COME HERE THIS MINUTE!'

Perfect Peter burst into tears. He jumped from the
chair and crept out of the room.

Horrid Henry sauntered over to the comfy black chair and stretched out. He picked up the remote and switched channels.

ZAP!

Rapper Zapper stormed into the spaceship and pulverized some alien slime.

'Way to go, Rapper Zapper!' shrieked Horrid Henry. Soon *Gross-Out* would be on. Wasn't life sweet?

Dear Mum and Dad
I want more pockit money and I want it now. Or else.
Henry
Henry
What have you done to deserve more pocket money?
Mum.
I didn't kick Peter today and I only called him Pongy-Pants and Mega-Stink twice. So I think I deserve a medal AND loads of loot
Henry

HORRID HENRY'S HOUSE

Stop calling me a worm.
And your room is smelly.

Not as smelly as you.

Meanie

Poo-breath

HORRID HENRY
AND THE
FANGMANGLER

orrid Henry snatched his skeleton bank and tried to twist open the trap door. Mum was taking him to Toy Heaven tomorrow. At last Henry would be able to buy the toy of his dreams: a Dungeon Drink kit. Ha ha ha – the tricks he'd play on his family, substituting their drinks for Dungeon stinkers.

Best of all, Moody Margaret would be green with envy. She wanted a Dungeon Drink kit too, but she didn't have any money. He'd have one first, and no way was Margaret ever going to play with it. Except for buying the occasional sweet and a few comics, Henry had been saving his money for weeks.

Perfect Peter peeked round the door.

'I've saved £7.53,' said Peter proudly, jingling his piggy bank.

'More than enough to buy my nature kit. How much do you have?'

'Millions,' said Henry.

Perfect Peter gasped.

'You do not,' said Peter. 'Do you?'

Henry shook his bank. A thin rattle came from within.

'That doesn't sound like millions,' said Peter.

'That's 'cause five pound notes don't rattle, stupid,' said Henry.

'Mum! Henry called me stupid,' shrieked Peter.

'Stop being horrid, Henry!' shouted Mum.

Horrid Henry gave the lid of his bank a final yank and spilled the contents on to the floor.

A single, solitary five pence coin rolled out.

Henry's jaw dropped. He grabbed the bank and fumbled around inside. It was empty.

'I've been robbed!' howled Horrid Henry. 'Where's my money? Who stole my money?'

Mum ran into the room.

'What's all this fuss?'

'Peter stole my money!' screamed Henry. He glared at his brother. 'Just wait until I get my hands on you, you little thief, I'll —'

'No one stole your money, Henry,' said Mum. 'You've spent it all on sweets and comics.'

'I have not!' shrieked Henry.

Mum pointed at the enormous pile of comics and sweet wrappers littering the floor of Henry's bedroom.

'What's all that then?' asked Mum.

Horrid Henry stopped shrieking. It was true. He *had* spent all his pocket money on comics and sweets. He just hadn't noticed.

'It's not fair!' he screamed.

'I saved all *my* pocket money, Mum,' said Perfect Peter. 'After all, a penny saved is a penny earned.'

Mum smiled at him. 'Well done, Peter. Henry, let this be a lesson to you.'

'I can't wait to buy my nature kit,' said Perfect Peter. 'You should have saved your money like I did, instead of wasting it, Henry.'

Henry growled and sprang at Peter. He was an Indian warrior scalping a settler.

'YOWWWW!' squealed Peter.

'Henry! Stop it!' shouted Mum. 'Say sorry to Peter.'

'I'm not sorry!' screamed Henry. 'I want my money!'

'Any more nonsense from you, young man, and we won't be going to Toy Heaven,' said Mum.

Henry scowled.

'I don't care,' he muttered. What was the point of going to Toy Heaven if he couldn't buy any toys?

Horrid Henry lay on his bedroom floor kicking sweet wrappers. That Dungeon Drink kit cost £4.99. He had to get some money by tomorrow. The question was, how?

He could steal Peter's money. That was tempting, as he knew the secret place in Peter's cello case where Peter hid his bank. Wouldn't that be fun when Peter discovered his money was gone? Henry smiled.

On second thoughts, perhaps not. Mum and Dad would be sure to suspect Henry, especially if he suddenly had money and Peter didn't.

He could sell some of his comics to Moody Margaret.

'No!' shrieked Henry, clutching his comics to his chest. Not his precious comics. There *had* to be another way.

Then Henry had a wonderful, spectacular idea. It was so superb that he did a wild war dance for joy. That Dungeon Drink kit was as good as his. And, better still, Peter would give him all the money he needed. Henry chortled. This would be as easy as taking sweets from a baby . . . and a lot more fun.

Horrid Henry strolled down the hall to Peter's room. Peter was having a meeting of the Best Boys Club (motto: Can I help?) with his friends Tidy Ted, Spotless Sam and Goody-Goody Gordon. What luck. More money for him. Henry smiled as he put his ear to the keyhole and listened to them discussing their good deeds.

'I helped an old lady cross the road *and* I ate all my vegetables,' said Perfect Peter.

'I kept my room tidy all week,' said Tidy Ted.

'I scrubbed the bath without being asked,' said Spotless Sam.

'I never once forgot to say please and thank you,' said Goody-Goody Gordon.

Henry pushed past the barricades and burst into Peter's room.

'Password!' screeched Perfect Peter.

'Vitamins,' said Horrid Henry.

'How did you know?' said Tidy Ted, staring open-mouthed at Henry.

'Never you mind,' said Henry, who was not a master spy for nothing. 'I don't suppose any of you know about Fangmanglers?'

The boys looked at one another.

'What are they?' asked Spotless Sam.

'Only the slimiest, scariest, most horrible and frightening monsters in the whole world,' said Henry. 'And I know where to find one.'

'Where?' said Goody-Goody Gordon.

'I'm not going to tell you,' said Horrid Henry.

'Oh please!' said Spotless Sam.

Henry shook his head and lowered his voice.

'Fangmanglers only come out at night,' whispered Henry. 'They slip into the shadows then sneak out and . . . BITE YOU!' he suddenly shrieked.

The Best Boys Club members gasped with fright.

'I'm not scared,' said Peter. 'And I've never heard of a Fangmangler.'

'That's because you're too young,' said Henry. 'Grown-ups don't tell you about them because they don't want to scare you.'

'I want to see it,' said Tidy Ted.

'Me too,' said Spotless Sam and Goody-Goody Gordon.

Peter hesitated for a moment.

'Is this a trick, Henry?'

'Of course not,' said Henry. 'And just for that I won't let you come.'

'Oh please, Henry,' said Peter.

Henry paused.

'All right,' he said. 'We'll meet in the back garden after dark. But it will cost you two pounds each.'

'Two pounds!' they squealed.

'Do you want to see a Fangmangler or don't you?'

Perfect Peter exchanged a look with his friends.

They all nodded.

'Good,' said Horrid Henry. 'See you at six o'clock. And don't forget to bring your money.'

Tee hee, chortled Henry silently. Eight pounds! He could get a Dungeon Drink kit *and* a Grisly Ghoul Grub box at this rate.

Loud screams came from next-door's garden.

'Give me back my spade!' came Moody Margaret's bossy tones.

'You're so mean, Margaret,' squealed Sour Susan's sulky voice. 'Well, I won't. It's my turn to dig with it now.'

WHACK! THWACK!

'WAAAAAAA!'

Eight pounds is nice, thought Horrid Henry, but twelve is even nicer.

'What's going on?' asked Horrid Henry, smirking as he leapt over the wall.

'Go away, Henry!' shouted Moody Margaret.

'Yeah, Henry,' echoed Sour Susan, wiping away her tears. 'We don't want you.'

'All right,' said Henry. 'Then I won't tell you about the Fangmangler I've found.'

'We don't want to know about it,' said Margaret, turning her back on him.

'That's right,' said Susan.

'Well then, don't blame me when the Fangmangler sneaks over the wall and rips you to pieces and chews up your guts,' said Horrid Henry. He turned to go.

The girls looked at one another.

'Wait,' ordered Margaret.

'Yeah?' said Henry.

'You don't scare me,' said Margaret.

'Prove it then,' said Henry.

'How?' said Margaret.

'Be in my garden at six o'clock tonight and I'll show you the Fangmangler. But it will cost you two pounds each.'

'Forget it,' said Margaret. 'Come on, Susan.'

'OK,' said Henry quickly. 'A pound each.'

'No,' said Margaret.

'And your money back if the Fangmangler doesn't scare you,' said Henry.

Moody Margaret smiled.

'It's a deal,' she said.

When the coast was clear, Horrid Henry crept into the bushes and hid a bag containing his supplies: an old, torn T-shirt, some filthy trousers and a jumbo-sized bottle of ketchup. Then he sneaked back into the house and waited for dark.

'Thank you, thank you, thank you, thank you,' said Horrid Henry, collecting two pounds from each member of the Best Boys Club. Henry placed the money carefully in his skeleton bank. Boy, was he rich!

Moody Margaret and Sour Susan handed over a pound each.

'Remember, Henry, we get our money back if we aren't scared,' hissed Moody Margaret.

'Shut up, Margaret,' said Henry. 'I'm risking my life

and all you can think about is money. Now everyone, wait here, don't move and don't talk,' he whispered. 'We have to surprise the Fangmangler. If not . . .' Henry paused and drew his fingers across his throat.

'I'm a goner. I'm going off now to hunt for the monster. When I find him, and if it's safe, I'll whistle twice. Then everyone come, as quietly as you can. But be careful!'

Henry disappeared into the black darkness of the garden.

For a long, long moment there was silence.

'This is stupid,' said Moody Margaret.

Suddenly, a low, moaning growl echoed through the moonless night.

'What was that?' said Spotless Sam nervously.

'Henry? Are you all right, Henry?' squeaked Perfect Peter.

The low moaning growl turned into a snarl.

THRASH! CRASH!

'HELP! HELP! THE FANGMANGLER'S AFTER ME! RUN FOR YOUR LIVES!' screamed Horrid Henry, smashing through the bushes. His T-shirt and trousers were torn. There was blood everywhere.

The Best Boys Club screamed and ran.

Sour Susan screamed and ran.

Moody Margaret screamed and ran.

Horrid Henry screamed and . . . stopped.

He waited until he was alone. Then Horrid Henry wiped some ketchup from his face, clutched his bank and did a war dance round the garden, whooping with joy.

'Money! Money! Money! Money! Money!' he squealed, leaping and stomping. He danced and he pranced, he twirled and he whirled. He was so busy dancing and cackling he didn't notice a shadowy shape slip into the garden behind him.

'Money! Money! Money! Mine! Mine –' he broke off. What was that noise? Horrid Henry's throat tightened.

Nah, he thought. It's nothing.

Then suddenly a dark shape leapt out of the bushes and let out a thunderous roar.

Horrid Henry shrieked with terror. He dropped his money and ran for his life. The Thing scooped up his bank and slithered over the wall.

Horrid Henry did not stop running until he was safely in his room with the door shut tight and barricaded. His heart pounded.

There really is a Fangmangler, he thought, trembling. And now it's after *me.*

Horrid Henry hardly slept a wink. He started awake at every squeak and creak. He shook and he shrieked. Henry had such a bad night that he slept in quite late the next morning, tossing and turning.

FIZZ! POP! GURGLE! BANG!

Henry jerked awake. What was that? He peeked his head out from under the duvet and listened.

FIZZ! POP! GURGLE! BANG!

Those fizzing and popping noises seemed to be coming from next door.

Henry ran to the window and pulled open the curtains. There was Moody Margaret sitting beside a large Toy Heaven bag. In front of her was . . .

a Dungeon Drink kit. She saw him, smiled, and raised a glass of bubbling black liquid.

'Want a Fangmangler drink, Henry?' asked Margaret sweetly.

❧ Dear Mum and Dad ❀

In case you forgot, it's my birthday in 2 months and 13 days.
I want lots of toys.
And, ^{LOTs of} money is always good
∧

Henry

P.s.   Vests, socks and books are NOT presents.

Dear Henry's Parents,
I am sorry to tell you that today Henry poked Brian, pinched Gurinder, made rude faces, broke Margaret's pencil, ate sweets in class, failed his maths test and did not hand in his homework.
Please come in and see me IMMEDIATELY!
Boudicca Battle-Axe

Sam
Would like t...
..... Pete
To his Birthd...
At
Our Town M...

Henry
Come to my
BIRTHDAY PARTY
At Lazer Zap
Toby

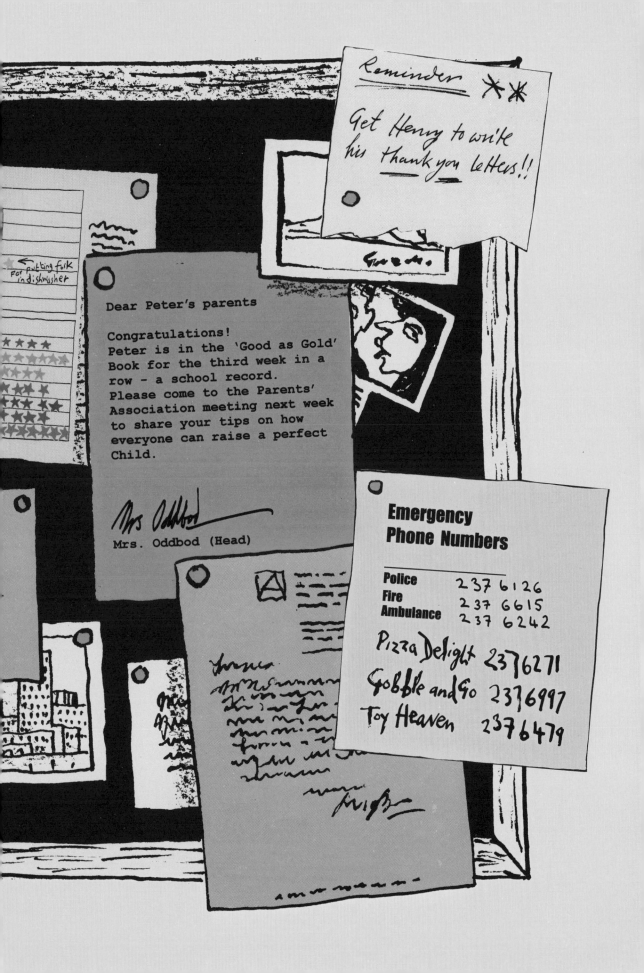

Stinky

Ugly! Pongy! Nappie-face! TOAD!

HORRID HENRY
TRICKS THE
TOOTH FAIRY

'It's not fair!' shrieked Horrid Henry. He trampled on Dad's new flower-bed, squashing the pansies. 'It's just not fair!'

Moody Margaret had lost two teeth. Sour Susan had lost three. Clever Clare lost two in one day. Rude Ralph had lost four, two top and two bottom, and could spit to the blackboard from his desk. Greedy Graham's teeth were pouring out. Even Weepy William had lost one – and that was ages ago.

Every day someone swaggered into school showing off a big black toothy gap and waving 50p or even a pound that the Tooth Fairy had brought. Everyone, that is, but Henry.

'It's not fair!' shouted Henry again. He yanked on his teeth. He pulled, he pushed, he tweaked, and he tugged.

They would not budge.

210

His teeth were superglued to his gums.

'Why me?' moaned Henry, stomping on the petunias. 'Why am I the only one who hasn't lost a tooth?'

Horrid Henry sat in his fort and scowled. He was sick and tired of other kids flaunting their ugly wobbly teeth and disgusting holes in their gums. The next person who so much as mentioned the word 'tooth' had better watch out.

'HENRY!' shouted a squeaky little voice. 'Where are you?'

Horrid Henry hid behind the branches.

'I know you're in the fort, Henry,' said Perfect Peter.

'Go away!' said Henry.

'Look, Henry,' said Peter. 'I've got something wonderful to show you.'

Henry scowled. 'What?'

'You have to see it,' said Peter.

Peter never had anything good to show. His idea of something wonderful was a new stamp, or a book about plants, or a gold star from his teacher saying how perfect he'd been. Still . . .

Henry crawled out.

'This had better be good,' he said. 'Or you're in big trouble.'

Peter held out his fist and opened it.

211

There was something small and white in Peter's hand. It looked like . . . no, it couldn't be.

Henry stared at Peter. Peter smiled as wide as he could. Henry's jaw dropped. This was impossible. His eyes must be playing tricks on him.

Henry blinked. Then he blinked again.

His eyes were not playing tricks. Perfect Peter, his *younger* brother, had a black gap at the bottom of his mouth where a tooth had been.

Henry grabbed Peter. 'You've coloured in your tooth with black crayon, you faker.'

'Have not!' shrieked Peter. 'It fell out. See.'

Peter proudly poked his finger through the hole in his mouth.

It was true. Perfect Peter had lost a tooth. Henry felt as if a fist had slammed into his stomach.

'Told you,' said Peter. He smiled again at Henry.

Henry could not bear to look at Peter's gappy teeth a second longer. This was the worst thing that had ever happened to him.

'I hate you!' shrieked Henry. He was a volcano
pouring hot molten lava on to the puny human
foolish enough to get in his way.

'AAAAGGGGHHHH!' screeched Peter, dropping
the tooth.

Henry grabbed it.

'OWWWW!' yelped Peter. 'Give me back my
tooth!'

'Stop being horrid, Henry!' shouted Mum.

Henry dangled the tooth in front of Peter.

'Nah nah ne nah nah,' jeered Henry.

Peter burst into tears.

'Give me back my tooth!' screamed Peter.

Mum ran into the garden.

'Give Peter his tooth this minute,' said Mum.

'No,' said Henry.

Mum looked fierce. She put out her hand. 'Give it
to me right now.'

Henry dropped the tooth on the ground.

'There,' said Horrid Henry.

'That's it, Henry,' said Mum. 'No pudding tonight.'

Henry was too miserable to care.

Peter scooped up his tooth. 'Look, Mum,' said Peter.

'My big boy!' said Mum, giving him a hug. 'How wonderful.'

'I'm going to use my money from the Tooth Fairy to buy some stamps for my collection,' said Peter.

'What a good idea,' said Mum.

Henry stuck out his tongue.

'Henry's sticking out his tongue at me,' said Peter.

'Stop it, Henry,' said Mum. 'Peter, keep that tooth safe for the Tooth Fairy.'

'I will,' said Peter. He closed his fist tightly round the tooth.

Henry sat in his fort. If a tooth wouldn't fall out, he would have to help it. But what to do? He could take a hammer and smash one out. Or he could tie string round a tooth, tie the string round a door handle and slam the door. Eek! Henry grabbed his jaw.

On second thoughts, perhaps not. Maybe there was

a less painful way of losing a tooth. What was it the dentist always said? Eat too many sweets and your teeth will fall out?

Horrid Henry sneaked into the kitchen. He looked to the right. He looked to the left. No one was there. From the sitting room came the screechy scratchy sound of Peter practising his cello.

Henry dashed to the cupboard where Mum kept the sweet jar. Sweet day was Saturday, and today was Thursday. Two whole days before he got into trouble.

Henry stuffed as many sticky sweets into his mouth as fast as he could.

Chomp Chomp Chomp Chomp.
Chomp Chew Chomp Chew.
Chompa Chew
Chompa Chew.
Chompa ...
Chompa ...
Chompa ...

Chompa ...

C h e w

Henry's jaw started to slow down. He put the last  sticky toffee in his mouth and forced his teeth to move up and down.

Henry started to feel sick. His teeth felt even sicker. He wiggled them hopefully. After all that sugar one was sure to fall out. He could see all the comics he would buy with his pound already.

Henry wiggled his teeth again. And again. Nothing moved.

Rats, thought Henry. His mouth hurt. His gums hurt. His tummy hurt. What did a boy have to do to get a tooth?

Then Henry had a wonderful, spectacular idea. It was so wonderful that he hugged himself. Why should Peter get a pound from the Tooth Fairy? Henry would get that pound, not him. And how? Simple. He would trick the Tooth Fairy.

The house was quiet. Henry tiptoed into Peter's room. There was Peter, sound asleep, a big smile on his face. Henry sneaked his hand under Peter's pillow and stole the tooth.

Tee hee, thought Henry. He tiptoed out of Peter's room and bumped into Mum.

'AAAAGGGGHH!' shrieked Henry.

'AAAAGGGGHH!' shrieked Mum.

'You scared me,' said Henry.

'What are you doing?' said Mum.

'Nothing,' said Henry. 'I thought I heard a noise in Peter's room and went to check.'

Mum looked at Henry. Henry tried to look sweet.

'Go back to bed, Henry,' said Mum.

Henry scampered to his room and put the tooth under his pillow. Phew. That was a close call. Henry smiled. Wouldn't that crybaby Peter be furious the next morning when he found no tooth and no money?

Henry woke up and felt under his pillow. The tooth was gone. Hooray, thought Henry. Now for the money.

Henry searched under the pillow.

Henry searched on top of the pillow.

He searched under the covers, under Teddy, under the bed, everywhere. There was no money.

Henry heard Peter's footsteps pounding down the hall.

'Mum, Dad, look,' said Peter. 'A whole pound from the Tooth Fairy!'

'Great!' said Mum.

'Wonderful!' said Dad.

What?! thought Henry.

'Shall I share it with you, Mum?' said Peter.

'Thank you, darling Peter, but no thanks,' said Mum. 'It's for you.'

'I'll have it,' said Henry. 'There are loads of comics I want to buy. And some –'

'No,' said Peter. 'It's mine. Get your own tooth.'

Henry stared at his brother. Peter would never have dared to speak to him like that before.

Horrid Henry pretended he was a pirate captain pushing a prisoner off the plank.

'OWWW!' shrieked Peter.

'Don't be horrid, Henry,' said Dad.

Henry decided to change the subject fast.

'Mum,' said Henry. 'How does the Tooth Fairy *know* who's lost a tooth?'

'She looks under the pillow,' said Mum.

'But how does she know whose pillow to look under?'

'She just does,' said Mum. 'By magic.'

'But how?' said Henry.

'She sees the gap between your teeth,' said Mum.

Aha, thought Henry. That's where he'd gone wrong.

That night Henry cut out a small piece of black paper, wet it, and covered over his two bottom teeth. He smiled at himself in the mirror. Perfect, thought Henry. He smiled again.

Then Henry stuck a pair of Dracula teeth under his pillow. He tied a string round the biggest tooth, and tied the string to his finger. When the Tooth Fairy came, the string would pull on his finger and wake him up.

All right, Tooth Fairy, thought Henry. You think you're so smart. Find your way out of this one.

The next morning was Saturday. Henry woke up and felt under his pillow. The string was still attached to his finger, but the Dracula teeth were gone. In their place was something small and round . . .

'My pound coin!' crowed Henry. He grabbed it.

The pound coin was plastic.

There must be some mistake, thought Henry. He checked under the pillow again. But all he found was a folded piece of bright blue paper, covered in stars.

Henry opened it. There, in tiny letters, he read:

Nice try Henry
The Tooth Fairy

'Rats,' said Henry.

From downstairs came the sound of Mum shouting.

'Henry! Get down here this minute!'

'What now?' muttered Henry, heaving his heavy bones out of bed.

'Yeah?' said Henry.

Mum help up an empty jar.

'Well?' said Mum.

Henry had forgotten all about the sweets.

'It wasn't me,' said Henry automatically. 'We must have mice.'

'No sweets for a month,' said Mum. 'You'll eat apples instead. You can start right now.'

Ugh. Apples. Henry hated all fruits and vegetables, but apples were the worst.

'Oh no,' said Henry.

'Oh yes,' said Mum. 'Right now.'

Henry took the apple and bit off the teeniest, tiniest piece he could.

CRUNCH.   CRACK.

Henry choked. Then he swallowed, gasping and spluttering.

His mouth felt funny. Henry poked around with his tongue and felt a space.

He shoved his fingers in his mouth, then ran to the mirror.

His tooth was gone.

He'd swallowed it.

'It's not fair!' shrieked Horrid Henry.

Dear Tooth Fairy

Dont you think it's time
to start bringing
£2 coins ?

Yor friend

Henry

Peter's Room

Henry's Room

Mum and Dad
Just to remind you, it's my birthday in 1 month and 7 days. I need a Rapper Zapper lunchbox! And a Terminater Gladiator sord and shield! And Siren Trainers with the flashing red lights! And the Intergalactic Samurai Gurillas which launch real Stinkbombs

~~If you don't buy them for me~~
~~You'll be very sorry~~
~~If you don't buy them for me~~
~~I'll be sorry~~
Buy them or else. Henry

HORRID HENRY GETS RICH QUICK

Horrid Henry loved money. He loved counting money. He loved holding money. He loved spending money. There was only one problem. Horrid Henry never had any money.

He sat on his bedroom floor and rattled his empty skeleton bank. How his mean parents expected him to get by on 50p a week pocket money he would never know. It was so unfair! Why should they have all the money when there were so many things *he* needed? Comic books. Whopper chocolate bars. A new football. More knights for his castle. Horrid Henry looked round his room, scowling. True, his shelves were filled with toys, but nothing he still wanted to play with.

'MUM!' screamed Henry.

'Stop shouting, Henry,' shouted Mum. 'If you have something to say come downstairs and say it.'

'I need more pocket money,' said Henry. 'Ralph gets a pound a week.'

'Different children get different amounts,' said Mum. 'I think 50p a week is perfectly adequate.'

'Well I don't,' said Henry.

'I'm very happy with *my* pocket money, Mum,' said Perfect Peter. 'I always save loads from my 30p. After all, if you look after the pennies the pounds will look after themselves.'

'Quite right, Peter,' said Mum, smiling.

Henry walked slowly past Peter. When Mum wasn't looking he reached out and grabbed him. He was a giant crab crushing a prawn in its claws.

'OWWW!' wailed Peter. 'Henry pinched me!'

'I did not,' said Henry.

'No pocket money for a week, Henry,' said Mum.

'That's not fair!' howled Henry. 'I need money!'

'You'll just have to save more,' said Mum.

'No!' shouted Henry. He hated saving money.

'Then you'll have to find a way to earn some,' said Mum.

Earn? Earn money? Suddenly Henry had a brilliant, fantastic idea.

'Mum, can I set up a stall and sell some stuff I don't want?'

'Like what?' said Mum.

'You know, old toys, comics, games, things I don't use any more,' said Henry.

Mum hesitated for a moment. She couldn't think of anything wrong with selling off old junk.

229

'All right,' said Mum.

'Can I help, Henry?' said Peter.

'No way,' said Henry.

'Oh please,' said Peter.

'Stop being horrid, Henry, and let Peter help you,' said Mum, 'or no stall.'

'OK,' said Henry, scowling, 'you can make the For Sale signs.'

Horrid Henry ran to his bedroom and piled his unwanted jumble into a box. He cleared his shelves of books, his wardrobe of party clothes, and his toybox of puzzles with pieces missing.

Then Horrid Henry paused. To make big money he definitely needed a few more valuable items. Now, where could he find some?

Henry crept into Peter's room. He could sell Peter's stamp collection, or his nature kit. Nah, thought Henry, no one would want that boring stuff.

Then Henry glanced inside Mum and Dad's room. It was packed with rich pickings. Henry sauntered over to Mum's dressing table. Look at all that perfume, thought Henry, she wouldn't miss one bottle. He chose a large crystal bottle with a swan-shaped stopper

and packed it in the box. Now, what other jumble could he find?

Aha! There was Dad's tennis racquet. Dad never played tennis. That racquet was just lying there collecting dust when it could go to a much better home.

Perfect, thought Henry, adding the racquet to his collection. Then he staggered out to the pavement to set up the display.

Horrid Henry surveyed his stall. It was piled high with great bargains. He should make a fortune.

'But Henry,' said Peter, looking up from drawing a sign, 'that's Dad's tennis racquet. Are you sure he wants you to sell it?'

'Of course I'm sure, stupid,' snapped Henry. If only he could get rid of his horrible brother, wouldn't life be perfect.

Then Horrid Henry looked at Peter. What was it

231

the Romans did with their leftover captives? Hmmn, he thought. He looked again. Hmmmn, he thought.

'Peter,' said Henry sweetly, 'would you like to earn some money?'

'Oh yes!' said Peter. 'How?'

'We could sell you as a slave.'

Perfect Peter thought for a moment.

'How much would I get?'

'10p,' said Henry.

'Wow,' said Peter. 'That means I'll have £6.47 in my piggybank. Can I wear a For Sale sign?'

'Certainly,' said Horrid Henry. He scribbled: For Sale £5, then placed the sign round Peter's neck.

'Now look smart,' said Henry. 'I see some customers coming.'

'What's going on?' said Moody Margaret.

'Yeah, Henry, what are you doing?' said Sour Susan.

'I'm having a jumble sale,' said Henry. 'Lots of

232

bargains. All the money raised will go to a very good cause.'

'What's that?' said Susan.

'Children in Need,' said Henry. I am a child and I'm certainly in need so that's true, he thought.

Moody Margaret picked up a punctured football.

'Bargain? This is just a lot of old junk.'

'No it isn't,' said Henry. 'Look. Puzzles, books, perfume, stuffed toys, *and* a slave.'

Moody Margaret looked up.

'I could use a good slave,' said Margaret. 'I'll give you 25p for him.'

'25p for an excellent slave? He's worth at least £1.50.'

'Make a muscle, slave,' said Moody Margaret.

Perfect Peter made a muscle.

'Hmmn,' said Margaret. '50p is my final offer.'

'Done,' said Horrid Henry. Why had he never thought of selling Peter before?

'How come I get 10p when I cost 50p?' said Peter.

'Shopkeeper's expenses,' said Henry. 'Now run along with your new owner.'

Business was brisk.

Rude Ralph bought some football cards.

Sour Susan bought Best Bear and Mum's perfume.

Beefy Bert bought a racing car with three wheels.

Then Aerobic Al jogged by.

'Cool racquet,' he said, picking up Dad's racquet and giving it a few swings. 'How much?'

'£10,' said Henry.

'I'll give you £2,' said Al.

£2! That was more money than Horrid Henry had ever had in his life! He was rich!

'Done,' said Henry.

Horrid Henry sat in the sitting room gazing happily at his stacks of money. £3.12! Boy, would that buy a lot of chocolate! Mum came into the room.

'Henry, have you seen my new perfume? You know, the one with the swan on top.'

'No,' said Henry. Yikes, he never thought she would notice.

'And where's Peter?' said Mum. 'I thought he was playing with you.'

'He's gone,' said Henry.

Mum stared at him.

'What do you mean, gone?'

'Gone,' said Henry, popping a crisp into his mouth. 'I sold him.'

'You did what?' whispered Mum. Her face was pale.

'You said I could sell anything I didn't want, and I certainly didn't want Peter, so I sold him to Margaret.'

Mum's jaw dropped.

'You go straight over to Margaret's and buy him back!' screamed Mum. 'You horrid boy! Selling your own brother!'

'But I don't want him back,' said Henry.

'No ifs or buts, Henry!' screeched Mum. 'You just get your brother back.'

'I can't afford to buy him,' said Horrid Henry. 'If you want him back you should pay for him.'

'HENRY!' bellowed Mum.

'All right,' grumbled Henry, getting to his feet. He sighed. What a waste of good money, he thought, climbing over the wall into Margaret's garden.

Margaret was lying by the paddling pool.

'SLAVE!' she ordered. 'I'm hot! Fan me!'

Perfect Peter came out of her house carrying a large fan.

He started to wave it in Moody Margaret's direction.

'Faster, slave!' said Margaret.

Peter fanned faster.

'Slower, slave!' said Margaret.

Peter fanned slower.

'Slave! A cool drink, and make it snappy!' ordered Margaret.

Horrid Henry followed Peter back into the kitchen.

'Henry!' squeaked Peter. 'Have you come to rescue me?'

'No,' said Henry.

'Please,' said Peter. 'I'll do anything. You can have the 10p.'

The cash register in Henry's head started to whirl.

'Not enough,' said Henry.

'I'll give you 50p. I'll give you £1. I'll give you £2,' said Peter. 'She's horrible. She's even worse than you.'

'Right, you can stay here for ever,' said Henry.

'Sorry, Henry,' said Perfect Peter. 'You're the best brother in the world. I'll give you all my money.'

Horrid Henry looked as if he were considering this offer.

'All right, wait here,' said Henry. 'I'll see what I can do.'

'Thank you, Henry,' said Peter.

Horrid Henry went back into the garden.

'Where's my drink?' said Margaret.

'My mum says I have to have Peter back,' said Henry.

Moody Margaret gazed at him.

'Oh yeah?'

'Yeah,' said Henry.

'Well I don't want to sell him,' said Margaret. 'I paid good money for him.'

Henry had hoped she'd forgotten that.

'OK, here's the 50p,' he said.

Moody Margaret lay back and closed her eyes.

'I haven't spent all this time and effort training him just to get my money back,' she said. 'He's worth at least £10 now.'

Slowly Henry stuck his hand back into his pocket.

'75p and that's my final offer.'

Moody Margaret knew a good deal when she was offered one.

'OK,' she said. 'Give me my money.'

Reluctantly, Henry paid her. But that still leaves over £2, thought Henry, so I'm well ahead.

Then he went in to fetch Peter.

'You cost me £6,' he said.

'Thank you, Henry,' said Peter. 'I'll pay you as soon as we get home.'

Yippee! thought Horrid Henry. I'm super rich! The world is mine!

Clink, clank, clink, went Henry's heavy pockets as Henry did his money dance.

 'CLINK, CLANK, CLINK,
I'm rich, I'm rich, I'm rich,
I'm rich as I can be,'

sang Henry.

Spend, spend, spend would be his motto from now on.

'Hello everybody,' called Dad, coming through the front door. 'What a lovely afternoon! Anyone for tennis?'

Horrid Henry's
Prized Possessions

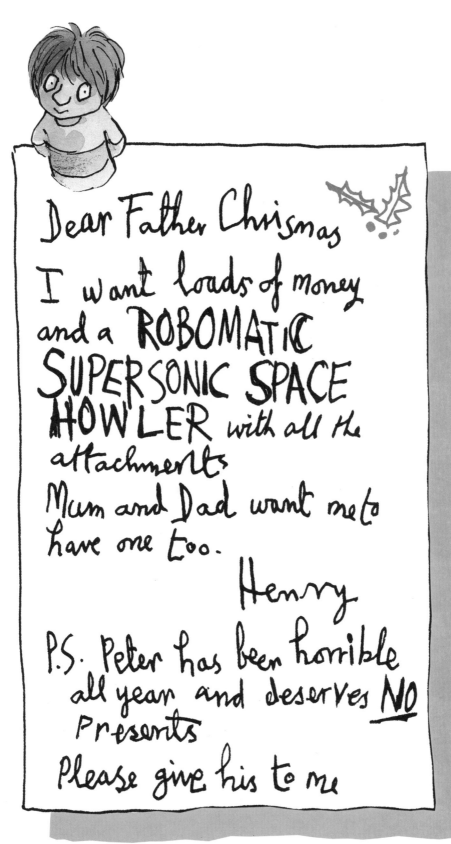

Dear Father Christmas

I want loads of money
and a ROBOMATIC
SUPERSONIC SPACE
HOWLER with all the
attachments
Mum and Dad want me to
have one too.

Henry

P.S. Peter has been horrible
all year and deserves **NO**
Presents
Please give his to me

I'm telling on you.

Tattle-tale

HORRID HENRY'S CHORES

The weekend! The lovely, lovely weekend. Sleeping in. Breakfast in his pyjamas. Morning TV. Afternoon TV. Evening TV. No school and no Miss Battle-Axe for two whole days.

In fact, there was only one bad thing about the weekend. Henry didn't even want to think about it. Maybe Mum would forget, he thought hopefully. Maybe today would be the day she didn't burst in and ruin everything.

Horrid Henry settled down in the comfy black chair and switched on his new favourite TV show, *Hog House*, where teenagers competed to see whose room was the most disgusting.

Henry couldn't wait till he was a terrible teen too. His bedroom would surely beat anything ever seen on *Hog House*.

'Eeeew,' squealed Horrid Henry happily, as Filthy Phil showed off what he kept under his bed.

'Yuck!' shrieked Horrid Henry, as Mouldy Myra yanked open her cupboard.

'Oooh, gross!' howled Horrid Henry, as Tornado Tariq showed why his family had moved out.

'And this week's winner for the most revolting room is –'

CLUNK

CLUNK

CLUNK

Mum clanked in. She was dragging her favourite instruments of torture: a hoover and a duster. Peter followed.

'Henry, turn off that horrid programme this minute,' said Mum. 'It's time to do your chores.'

'NO!' screamed Horrid Henry.

Was there a more hateful, horrible word in the world than chores? *Chores* was worse than *homework*. Worse than *vegetables*. Even worse than *injection, share,* and *bedtime*. When he was King no child would ever have to do chores. Any parent who so much as whispered the word *chores* would get catapulted over the battlements into the piranha-infested moat.

'You can start by picking up your dirty socks from the floor,' said Mum.

Pick up a sock? Pick up a sock? Was there no end to Mum's meanness? Who cared if he had a few old socks scattered around the place?

'I can't believe you're making me do this!' screamed Henry. He glared at Mum. Then he glared at his crumpled socks. The socks were miles away from the sofa. He'd pick them up later. Much later.

'Henry, your turn to hoover the sitting room,' said Mum. 'Peter, your turn to dust.'

'No!' howled Horrid Henry. 'I'm allergic to hoovers.'

Mum ignored him.

'Then empty the bins and put the dirty clothes into the washing machine. And make sure you separate the whites from the coloureds.'

Henry didn't move.

'It will only take fifteen minutes,' said Mum.

'It's not fair!' wailed Henry. 'I hoovered last week.'

'No you didn't, I did,' said Peter.

'I did!' screamed Henry. 'Liar!'

'Liar!'

'Can't I do it later?' said Horrid Henry. Later had such a happy way of turning into never.

'N-O spells no,' said Mum.

Peter started dusting the TV.

'Stop it!' said Henry. 'I'm watching.'

'I'm dusting,' said Peter.'

246

'Out of my way, worm,' hissed Horrid Henry.

Mum marched over and switched off the TV. 'No TV until you do your chores, Henry. Everyone has to pitch in and help in this family.'

Horrid Henry was outraged. Why should he help around the house? That was his lazy parents' job. Didn't he work hard enough already, heaving his heavy bones to school every day?

And all the schoolwork he did! It was amazing, thought Horrid Henry, as he lay kicking and screaming on the sofa, that he was still alive.

'I WON'T! I'M NOT YOUR SLAVE!'

'Henry, it's not fair if Mum and Dad do *all* the housework,' said Perfect Peter.

That seemed fair to Henry.

'Quite right, Peter,' said Mum, beaming. 'What a lovely thoughtful boy you are.'

'Shut up, Peter!' screamed Henry.

'Don't be horrid, Henry!' screamed Mum.

'No TV and no pocket money until you do your chores,' said Dad, running in.

Henry stopped screaming.

No pocket money! No TV!

'I don't need any pocket money,' shrieked Henry.

'Fine,' said Mum.

Wait, what was he saying?

Of course he needed pocket money. How else would he buy sweets? And he'd die if he couldn't watch TV.

'I'm calling the police,' said Horrid Henry. 'They'll come and arrest you for child cruelty.'

'Finished!' sang out Perfect Peter. 'I've done all *my* chores,' he added, 'can I have my pocket money please?'

'Of course you can,' said Mum. She handed Peter a shiny 50p piece.

Horrid Henry glared at Peter. Could that ugly toad get any uglier?

'All right,' snarled Henry. 'I'll hoover. And out of my way, frog face, or I'll hoover you up.'

'Mum!' wailed Peter. 'Henry's trying to hoover me.'

'Just do your chores, Henry,' said Mum. She felt tired.

'You could have done *all* your chores in the time you've spent arguing,' said Dad. He felt tired, too.

Henry slammed the sitting room door behind his mean, horrible parents. He looked at the hoover with loathing. Why didn't that stupid machine just hoover by itself? A robot hoover, that's what he needed.

Henry switched it on.

VROOM!   VROOM!

'Hoover, hoover!' ordered Henry.

The hoover did not move.

'Go on, hoover, you can do it,' said Henry.

VROOM!   VROOM!

Still the hoover didn't move.

What a lot of noise that stupid machine makes, thought Henry. I bet you can hear it all over the house.

And then suddenly Horrid Henry had a brilliant, spectacular idea. Why had he never thought of it before? He'd ask to hoover every week.

Henry dragged the hoover over to the sitting room door and left it roaring there. Then he flopped on the sofa and switched on the TV. Great, *Hog House* hadn't finished!

Mum and Dad listened to the hoover blaring from the sitting room. Goodness, Henry was working hard. They were amazed.

'Isn't Henry doing a good job,' said Mum.

'He's been working over thirty minutes non-stop,' said Dad.

'Finally, he's being responsible,' said Mum.

'At last,' said Dad.

'Go Tariq!' cheered Henry, as Tornado Tariq blew into his parents' tidy bedroom. Ha ha ha, chortled Henry, what a shock those parents would get.

'Stay tuned for the Filthy Final between Tariq and Myra, coming up in three minutes!' said the presenter, Dirty Dirk.

Footsteps. Yikes, someone was coming.

Oh no.

Henry sprang from the sofa, turned off the telly and grabbed the hoover.

Mum walked in.

Horrid Henry began to pant.

'I've worked so hard, Mum,' gasped Henry. 'Please can I stop now?'

Mum stared at the dustballs covering the carpet.

'But Henry,' said Mum. 'There's still dust everywhere.'

'I can't help it,' said Henry. 'I did my best.'

'All right, Henry,' said Mum, sighing.

YES! thought Horrid Henry.

'But remember, no TV until you've emptied the bins and separated the laundry.'

'I know, I know,' muttered Henry, running up the stairs. If he finished his chores in the next two minutes, he'd be in time for the *Hog House* final!

Right. Mum said to empty the bins. She didn't say into what, just that the bins had to be empty.

It was the work of a few moments to tip all the wastepaper baskets onto the floor.

That's done, thought Horrid Henry, racing down the stairs. Now that stupid laundry. When he was a billionaire computer game tester, he'd never wash his clothes. He'd just buy new ones.

Horrid Henry glared at the dirty clothes piled on the floor in front of the washing machine. It would take him hours to separate the whites from the coloureds. What a waste of valuable time, thought Henry. Mum and Dad just made him do it to be mean. What difference could it make to wash a red sweatshirt with a white sheet? None.

Horrid Henry shoved all the clothes into the washing machine and slammed the door.

Free at last.

'Done!' shrieked Horrid Henry.

Wow, what a brilliant *Hog House* that was, thought Horrid Henry, jingling his pocket money. He wandered past the washing machine. Strange, he didn't remember all those pink clothes swirling around. Since when did his family have pink sheets and pink towels?

Since he'd washed a red sweatshirt with the whites. Uh oh.

Mum would be furious. Dad would be furious. His punishment would be terrible. Hide! thought Horrid Henry.

Dad stared at his newly pink underpants, shirts, and vests.

Mum stared at her best white skirt, now her worst pink one.

Henry stared at the floor. This time there was no escape.

'Maybe we're asking too much of you,' said Dad, gazing at the trail of rubbish lying round the house.

'You're just not responsible enough,' said Mum.

'Too clumsy,' said Dad.

'Too young,' said Mum.

'Maybe it's easier if we do the chores ourselves,' said Dad.

'Maybe it is,' said Mum.

Horrid Henry could hardly believe his ears. No more chores? Because he was so bad at doing them?

'Yippee!' squealed Henry.

'On the other hand, maybe not,' said Dad, glaring. 'We'll see how well you do your chores next week.'

'OK,' said Horrid Henry agreeably.

He had the feeling his chore-doing skills wouldn't be improving.

Horrid Henry's Chores

CHORES

	week 1	week 2	week 3	week 4
Hoover sitting room	~~Henry~~ **Peter**	Peter	~~Henry~~ **Peter**	Peter
Dust	~~Henry~~ **Peter**	Peter	~~Henry~~ **Peter**	Peter
Empty bins	~~Henry~~ **Peter**	Peter	~~Henry~~ **Peter**	Peter
Wash Clothes	Peter	~~Henry~~ **Peter**	Peter	~~Henry~~ **Peter**

Dear Mum and Dad
My birthday is next week!
Just so you know, everyone
got better presents than I
did last year. Ralph got a
Mutant Max T.shirt and a
Terminater Gladiator sord
shield, helmet <u>and</u> aKe.
<u>And</u> his parents always
buy him Siren Trainers.
<u>And</u> give him loads and loads
of cash
                    Henry

HORRID HENRY TRICKS AND TREATS

allowe'en! Oh happy, happy day! Every year Horrid Henry could not believe it: an entire day devoted to stuffing your face with sweets and playing horrid tricks. Best of all, you were *supposed* to stuff your face and play horrid tricks. Whoopee!

Horrid Henry was armed and ready. He had loo roll. He had water pistols. He had shaving foam. Oh my, would he be playing tricks tonight. Anyone who didn't instantly hand over a fistful of sweets would get it with the foam. And woe betide any fool who gave him an apple. Horrid Henry knew how to treat rotten grown-ups like that.

His red and black devil costume lay ready on the bed, complete with evil mask, twinkling horns, trident, and whippy tail. He'd scare everyone wearing that.

'Heh heh heh,' said Horrid Henry, practising his evil laugh.

'Henry,' came a little voice outside his bedroom door, 'come and see my new costume.'

'No,' said Henry.

'Oh please, Henry,' said his younger brother, Perfect Peter.

'No,' said Henry. 'I'm busy.'

'You're just jealous because *my* costume is nicer than yours,' said Peter.

'Am not.'

'Are too.'

Come to think of it, what *was* Peter wearing? Last year he'd copied Henry's monster costume and ruined Henry's Hallowe'en. What if he were copying Henry's devil costume? That would be just like that horrible little copycat.

'All right, you can come in for two seconds,' said Henry.

A big, pink bouncy bunny bounded into Henry's room. It had little white bunny ears. It had a little white bunny tail. It had pink polka dots everywhere else. Horrid Henry groaned. What a stupid costume. Thank goodness *he* wasn't wearing it.

'Isn't it great?' said Perfect Peter.

'No,' said Henry. 'It's horrible.'

'You're just saying that to be mean, Henry,' said Peter, bouncing up and down. 'I can't wait to go trick-or-treating in it tonight.'

Oh no. Horrid Henry felt as if he'd been punched in the stomach. Henry would be expected to go out trick or treating – with Peter! He, Henry, would have to walk around with a pink polka dot bunny. Everyone would see him. The shame of it! Rude Ralph would never stop teasing him. Moody Margaret would call him a bunny wunny. How could he play tricks on people with a pink polka dot bunny following him everywhere? He was ruined. His name would be a joke.

'You can't wear that,' said Henry desperately.

'Yes I can,' said Peter.

'I won't let you,' said Henry.

Perfect Peter looked at Henry. 'You're just jealous.'

Grrr! Horrid Henry was about to tear that stupid costume off Peter when, suddenly, he had an idea.

It was painful.

It was humiliating.

But anything was better than having Peter prancing about in pink polka dots.

'Tell you what,' said Henry, 'just because I'm so nice I'll let you borrow my monster costume. You've always wanted to wear it.'

'NO!' said Peter. 'I want to be a bunny.'

'But you're supposed to be scary for Hallowe'en,' said Henry.

'I am scary,' said Peter. 'I'm going to bounce up to people and yell "boo".'

'I can make you really scary, Peter,' said Horrid Henry.

'How?' said Peter.

'Sit down and I'll show you.' Henry patted his desk chair.

'What are you going to do?' said Peter suspiciously. He took a step back.

'Nothing,' said Henry. 'I'm just trying to help you.'

Perfect Peter didn't move.

'How can I be scarier?' he said cautiously.

'I can give you a scary haircut,' said Henry.

Perfect Peter clutched his curls.

'But I like my hair,' he said feebly.

'This is Hallowe'en,' said Henry. 'Do you want to be scary or don't you?'

'Um, um, uh,' said Peter, as Henry pushed him down in the chair and got out the scissors.

'Not too much,' squealed Peter.

'Of course not,' said Horrid Henry. 'Just sit back and relax, I promise you'll love this.'

Horrid Henry twirled the scissors.

Snip! Snip! Snip! Snip! Snip!

Magnificent, thought Horrid Henry. He gazed proudly at his work. Maybe he should be a hairdresser when he grew up. Yes! Henry could see it now. Customers would queue for miles for one of Monsieur Henri's scary snips. Shame his genius was wasted on someone as yucky as Peter. Still . . .

'You look great, Peter,' said Henry. 'Really scary. Atomic Bunny. Go and have a look.'

Peter went over and looked in the mirror.

'AAAAAAAAAARGGGGGGG!'

'Scared yourself, did you?' said Henry. 'That's great.'

'AAAAAAAAAARGGGGGGG!' howled Peter.

Mum ran into the room.

'AAAAAAAAAARGGGGGGG!' howled Mum.

'AAAAAAAAAARGGGGGGG!' howled Peter.

'Henry!' screeched Mum. 'What have you done! You horrid, horrid boy!'

What was left of Peter's hair stuck up in ragged tufts

263

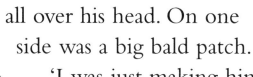

all over his head. On one side was a big bald patch.

'I was just making him look scary,' protested Henry. 'He said I could.'

'Henry made me!' said Peter.

'My poor baby,' said Mum. She glared at Henry.

'No trick-or-treating for you,' said Mum. 'You'll stay here.'

Horrid Henry could hardly believe his ears. This was the worst thing that had ever happened to him.

'NO!' howled Henry. This was all Peter's fault.

'I hate you, Peter!' he screeched. Then he attacked. He was Medusa, coiling round her victim with her snaky hair.

'Aaaahh!' screeched Peter.

'Henry!' shouted Mum. 'Go to your room!'

Mum and Peter left the house to go trick-or-treating. Henry had screamed and sobbed and begged. He'd put on his devil costume, just in case his tears melted their stony hearts. But no. His mean, horrible parents wouldn't change their mind. Well, they'd be sorry. They'd all be sorry.

Dad came into the sitting room. He was holding a large shopping bag.

'Henry, I've got some work to finish so I'm going to let you hand out treats to any trick-or-treaters.'

Horrid Henry stopped plotting his revenge. Had Dad gone mad? Hand out treats? What kind of punishment was this?

Horrid Henry fought to keep a big smile off his face.

'Here's the Hallowe'en stuff, Henry,' said Dad. He handed Henry the heavy bag. 'But remember,' he added sternly, 'these treats are not for you: they're to give away.'

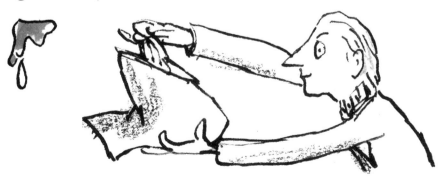

Yeah, right, thought Henry.

'OK, Dad,' he said as meekly as he could. 'Whatever you say.'

Dad went back to the kitchen. Now was his chance! Horrid Henry leapt on the bag. Wow, was it full! He'd grab all the good stuff, throw back anything yucky with lime or peppermint, and he'd have enough sweets to keep him going for at least a week!

Henry yanked open the bag. A terrible sight met his eyes. The bag was full of satsumas. And apples. And walnuts in their shells. No wonder his horrible parents had trusted him to be in charge of it.

Ding dong.

Slowly, Horrid Henry heaved his heavy bones to the door. There was his empty, useless trick-or-treat bag, sitting forlornly by the entrance.

Henry gave it a kick, then opened the door and glared.

'Whaddya want?' snapped Horrid Henry.

'Trick-or-treat,' whispered Weepy William. He was dressed as a pirate.

Horrid Henry held out the bag of horrors.

'Lucky dip!' he announced.

'Close your eyes for a big surprise!'

William certainly would be surprised at what a rotten treat he'd be getting.

Weepy William put down his swag bag, closed his eyes tight, then plunged his hand into Henry's lucky dip. He rummaged and he rummaged and he rummaged, hoping to find something better than satsumas.

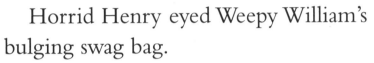

Horrid Henry eyed Weepy William's bulging swag bag.

Go on, Henry, urged the bag. He'll never notice.

Horrid Henry did not wait to be asked twice.

Horrid Henry grabbed a big handful of William's sweets and popped them inside his empty bag.

Weepy William opened his eyes.

'Did you take some of my sweets?'

'No,' said Henry.

William peeked inside his bag and burst into tears.

'Waaaaaaaa!' wailed William. 'Henry took –'

Henry pushed him out and slammed the door.

Dad came running.

'What's wrong?'

'Nothing,' said Henry. 'Just William crying 'cause he's scared of pumpkins.'

Phew, thought Henry. That was close. Perhaps he had been a little too greedy.

Ding dong.

It was Lazy Linda wearing a pillowcase over her head. 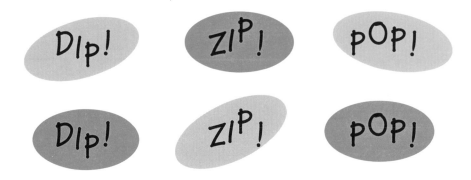 Gorgeous Gurinder was with her, dressed as a scarecrow.

'Trick-or-treat!'

'Trick-or-treat!'

'Close your eyes for a big surprise!' said Henry, holding out the lucky dip bag.

'Ooh, a lucky dip!' squealed Linda.

Lazy Linda and Gorgeous Gurinder put down their bags, closed their eyes, and reached into the lucky dip.

DIp!   ZIP!   pOP!

DIp!   ZIP!   pOP!

Lazy Linda opened her eyes.

'You give the worst treats ever, Henry,' said Linda, gazing at her walnut in disgust.

'We won't be coming back *here*,' sniffed Gorgeous Gurinder.

Tee hee, thought Horrid Henry.

Ding dong.

It was Beefy Bert. He was wearing a robot costume.

'Hi, Bert, got any good sweets?' asked Henry.

'I dunno,' said Beefy Bert.

Horrid Henry soon found out that he did. Lots and lots and lots of them. So did Moody Margaret, Sour Susan, Jolly Josh and Tidy Ted. Soon Henry's bag was stuffed with treats.

Ding dong.

Horrid Henry opened the door.

'Boo,' said Atomic Bunny.

Henry's sweet bag! Help! Mum would see it!

'Eeeeek!' screeched Horrid Henry. 'Help! Save me!'

Quickly, he ran upstairs clutching his bag and hid it safely under his bed. Phew, that was close.

'Don't be scared, Henry, it's only me,' called Perfect Peter.

Horrid Henry came back downstairs.

'No!' said Henry. 'I'd never have known.'

'Really?' said Peter.

'Really,' said Henry.

'Everyone just gave sweets this year,' said Perfect Peter. 'Yuck.'

Horrid Henry held out the lucky dip.

'Ooh, a satsuma,' said Peter. 'Aren't I lucky!'

'I hope you've learned your lesson, Henry,' said Mum sternly.

'I certainly have,' said Horrid Henry, eyeing Perfect Peter's bulging bag. 'Good things come to those who wait.'

SHOPPING LIST

Muesli
Carrots
Wholemeal Bread
Spinach
Eggs
Chicken
Raisins
Pickeled Union Crisps
Chocolit eyeballs
Chocolit cake
Crunchy crakkers
Sweet Tweets
Jumbo Pack of Big Boppers

HORRiD HENRY
AND THE
MUMMY'S CURSE

iptoe. Tiptoe. Tiptoe.

Horrid Henry crept down the hall. The coast was clear. Mum and Dad were in the garden, and Peter was playing at Tidy Ted's.

Tee hee, thought Henry, then darted into Perfect Peter's room and shut the door.

There it was. Sitting unopened on Peter's shelf. The grossest, yuckiest, most stomach-curdling kit Henry had ever seen. A brand-new, deluxe Curse of the Mummy kit, complete with a plastic body to mummify, mummy-wrapping gauze, curse book, amulets and, best of all, removable mummy organs to put in a canopic jar. Peter had won it at the 'Meet a Real Mummy' exhibition at the museum, but he'd never even played with it once.

Of course, Henry wasn't allowed into Peter's
bedroom without permission. He was also not allowed
to play with Peter's toys. This was so unfair, Henry
could hardly believe it. True, he wouldn't let Peter
touch his Boom-Boom Basher, his Goo-Shooter, or
his Dungeon Drink kit. In fact, since Henry refused
to share *any* of his toys with Peter, Mum had forbid-
den Henry to play with any of Peter's toys – or else.

Henry didn't care – Perfect Peter had boring baby
toys – until, that is, he brought home the mummy kit.
Henry had ached to play with it. And now was his
chance.

Horrid Henry tore off the wrapping, and opened
the box.

WOW! So gross! Henry felt a delicious shiver. He
loved mummies. What could be more thrilling than
looking at an ancient, wrapped-up DEAD body? Even
a pretend one was wonderful. And now he had hours
of fun ahead of him.

Pitter-patter! Pitter-patter! Pitter-patter!

Oh help, someone was coming up the stairs! Horrid Henry shoved the mummy kit behind him as Peter's bedroom door swung open and Perfect Peter strolled in.

'Out of my way, worm!' shouted Henry.

Perfect Peter slunk off. Then he stopped.

'Wait a minute,' he said. 'You're in *my* room! You can't order me out of my own room!'

'Oh yeah?' blustered Henry.

'Yeah!' said Peter.

'You're supposed to be at Ted's,' said Henry, trying to distract him.

'He got sick,' said Peter. He stepped closer. 'And you're playing with my kit! You're not allowed to play with any of my things! Mum said so! I'm going to tell her right now!'

Uh oh. If Peter told on him Henry would be in big trouble. Very big trouble. Henry had to save himself, fast. He had two choices. He could leap on Peter and throttle him. Or he could use weasel words.

'I wasn't playing with it,' said Henry smoothly. 'I was trying to protect you.'

'No you weren't,' said Peter. 'I'm telling.'

'I was, too,' said Henry. 'I was trying to protect you from the Mummy's Curse.'

Perfect Peter headed for the door. Then he stopped.

'What curse?' said Peter.

'The curse which turns people into mummies!' said Henry desperately.

'There's no such thing,' said Peter.

'Wanna bet?' said Henry. 'Everyone knows about the mummy's curse! They take on the shape of someone familiar but really, they're mummies! They could be your cat –'

'Fluffy?' said Peter. 'Fluffy, a mummy?'

Henry looked at fat Fluffy snoring peacefully on a cushion.

277

'Even Fluffy,' said Henry. 'Or Dad. Or me. Or you.'

'I'm not a mummy,' said Peter.

'Or even –' Henry paused melodramatically and then whispered, 'Mum.'

'Mum, a mummy?' gasped Peter.

'Yup,' said Henry. 'But don't worry. You help me draw some Eyes of Horus. They'll protect us against . . . her.'

'She's not a mummy,' said Peter.

'That's what she wants us to think,' whispered Henry. 'It's all here in the Mummy curse book.' He waved the book in front of Peter. 'Don't you think the mummy on the cover resembles you-know-who?'

'No,' said Peter.

'Watch,' said Horrid Henry. He grabbed a pencil.

'Don't draw on a book!' squeaked Peter.

Henry ignored him and drew glasses on the mummy.

'How about now?' he asked.

Peter stared. Was it his imagination or did the mummy look a little familiar?

'I don't believe you,' said Peter. 'I'm going straight down to ask Mum.'

'But that's the worst thing you could do!' shouted Henry.

'I don't care,' said Peter. Down he went.

Henry was sunk. Mum would probably cancel his birthday party when Peter blabbed. And he'd never even had a chance to play with the mummy kit! It was so unfair.

Mum was reading on the sofa.

'Mum,' said Peter, 'Henry says you're a mummy.'

Mum looked puzzled.

'Of course I'm a mummy,' she said.

'What?' said Peter.

'I'm your mummy,' said Mum, with a smile.

Peter took a step back.

'I don't want you to be a mummy,' said Peter.

'But I am one,' said Mum. 'Now come and give me a hug.'

'No!' said Peter.

'Let me wrap my arms around you,' said Mum.

'NO WRAPPING!' squealed Peter. 'I want my mummy!'

'But I'm your mummy,' said Mum.

'I know!' squeaked Peter. 'Keep away, you . . . mummy!'

Perfect Peter staggered up the stairs to Henry.

'It's true,' he gasped. 'She said she was a mummy.'

'She did?' said Henry.

'Yes,' said Peter. 'What are we going to do?'

'Don't worry, Peter,' said Henry. 'We can free her from the curse.'

'How?' breathed Peter.

Horrid Henry pretended to consult the curse book.

'First we must sacrifice to the Egyptian gods Osiris and Hroth,' said Henry.

'Sacrifice?' said Peter.

'They like cat guts, and stuff like that,' said Henry.

'No!' squealed Peter. 'Not . . . Fluffy!'

'However,' said Henry, leafing through the curse book, 'marbles are also acceptable as an offering.'

Perfect Peter ran to his toybox and scooped up a handful of marbles.

'Now fetch me some loo roll,' added Henry.

'Loo roll?' said Peter.

'Do not question the priest of Anubis!' shrieked Henry.

Perfect Peter fetched the loo roll.

'We must wrap Fluffy in the sacred bandages,' said Henry. 'He will be our messenger between this world and the next.'

'Meoww,' said Fluffy, as he was wrapped from head to tail in loo paper.

'Now you,' said Henry.

'Me?' squeaked Peter.

'Yes,' said Henry. 'Do you want to free Mum from the mummy's curse?'

Peter nodded.

'Then you must stand still and be quiet for thirty minutes,' said Henry. That should give him plenty of time to have a go with the mummy kit.

He started wrapping Peter. Round and round and round and round went the loo roll until Peter was tightly trussed from head to toe.

Henry stepped back to admire his work. Goodness, he was a brilliant mummy-maker! Maybe that's what he should be when he grew up. Henry, the Mummy-Maker. Henry, World's Finest Mummy-Maker. Henry, Mummy-Maker to the Stars. Yes, it certainly had a ring to it.

'You're a fine-looking mummy, Peter,' said Henry. 'I'm sure you'll be made very welcome in the next world.'

'Huuunh?' said Peter.

'Silence!' ordered Henry. 'Don't move. Now I must utter the sacred spell. By the powers of Horus, Morus, Borus and Stegosaurus,' intoned Henry, making up all the Egyptian sounding names he could.

'Stegosaurus?' mumbled Peter.

'Whatever!' snapped Henry. 'I call on the scarab! I call on Isis! Free Fluffy from the mummy's curse. Free Peter from the mummy's curse. Free Mum from the mummy's curse. Free –'

'What on earth is going on in here?' shrieked Mum, bursting through the door. 'You horrid boy! What have you done to Peter? And what have you done to poor Fluffy?'

'Meoww,' yowled Fluffy.

'Mummy!' squealed Perfect Peter.

284

MEOWW

Eowww, gross! thought Horrid Henry, opening up the plastic mummy body and placing the organs in the canopic jar.

The bad news was that Henry had been banned from watching TV for a week. The good news was that Perfect Peter had said he never wanted to see that horrible mummy kit again.

BABY  PICTURES

HORRID HENRY'S
BIRTHDAY PARTY

ebruary was Horrid Henry's favourite month.

His birthday was in February.

'It's my birthday soon!' said Henry every day after Christmas. 'And my birthday party! Hurray!'

February was Horrid Henry's parents' least favourite month.

'It's Henry's birthday soon,' said Dad, groaning.

'And his birthday party,' said Mum, groaning even louder.

Every year they thought Henry's birthday parties could not get worse. But they always did.

Every year Henry's parents said they would never ever let Henry have a birthday party again. But every year they gave Henry one absolutely last final chance.

Henry had big plans for this year's party.

'I want to go to Lazer Zap,' said Henry. He'd been to Lazer Zap for Tough Toby's party. They'd had a great time dressing up as spacemen and blasting each other in dark tunnels all afternoon.

'NO!' said Mum. 'Too violent.'

'I agree,' said Dad.

'And too expensive,' said Mum.

'I agree,' said Dad.

There was a moment's silence.

'However,' said Dad, 'it does mean the party wouldn't be here.'

Mum looked at Dad. Dad looked at Mum.

'How do I book?' said Mum.

'Hurray!' shrieked Henry. 'Zap! Zap! Zap!'

Horrid Henry sat in his fort holding a pad of paper. On the front cover in big capital letters Henry wrote:

Henry's Party Plans
Top Secret!

At the top of the first page Henry wrote:

Guests

A long list followed. Then Henry stared at the names and chewed his pencil.

Actually, I don't want Margaret, thought Henry. Too moody.

He crossed out Moody Margaret's name.

And I definitely don't want Susan. Too crabby.

In fact, I don't want any girls at all, thought Henry. He crossed out Clever Clare and Lazy Linda.

Then there was Anxious Andrew.

Nope, thought Henry, crossing him off. He's no fun.

Toby was possible, but Henry didn't really like him. Out went Tough Toby.

William?

No way, thought Henry. He'll be crying the second he gets zapped.

Out went Weepy William.

Ralph?

Henry considered. Ralph would be good because he was sure to get into trouble. On the other hand, he hadn't invited Henry to *his* party.

Rude Ralph was struck off.

So were Babbling Bob, Jolly Josh, Greedy Graham and Dizzy Dave. And absolutely no way was Peter coming anywhere near him on his birthday.

Ahh, that was better. No horrid kids would be coming to *his* party.

Henry's Party Plans
TOP SECRET

Guests

~~Margaret~~
~~Susan~~
~~Clare~~
~~Linda~~
~~Andrew~~
~~Toby~~
~~William~~
~~Ralph~~
~~Bob~~
~~Josh~~
~~Graham~~
~~Dave~~
~~Peter~~

There was only one problem. Every single name was crossed off.

No guests meant no presents.

Henry looked at his list. Margaret was a moody old grouch and he hated her, but she did sometimes give good gifts. He still had the jumbo box of day-glo slime she'd given him last year.

And Toby *had* invited Henry to *his* party.

And Dave was always spinning round like a top, falling and knocking things over which was fun. Graham would eat too much and burp. And Ralph was sure to say rude words and make all the grown-ups angry.

Oh, let them all come, thought Henry. Except Peter, of course. The more guests I have, the more presents I get!

Henry turned to the next page and wrote:

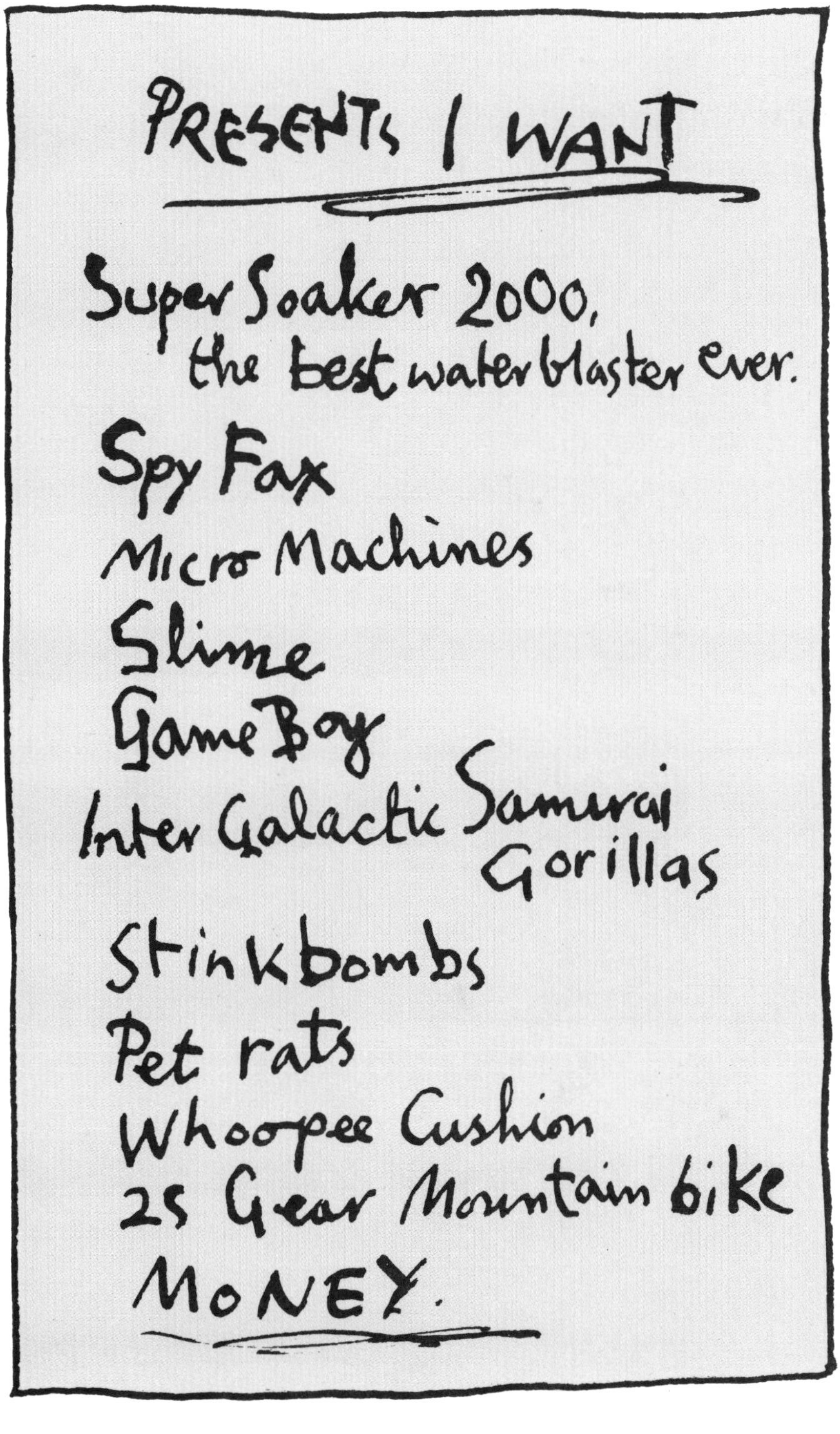

PRESENTS I WANT

Super Soaker 2000, the best water blaster ever.

Spy Fax

Micro Machines

Slime

Game Boy

Inter Galactic Samurai Gorillas

Stink bombs

Pet rats

Whoopee Cushion

25 Gear Mountain bike

MONEY.

He'd leave the list lying around where Mum and Dad were sure to find it.

'I've done the menu for the party,' said Mum. 'What do you think?'

Mum's Menu

carrot sticks
cucumber sandwiches
grapes
raisins
apple juice
carrot cake

'Blecccccch,' said Henry. 'I don't want that horrible food at my party. I want food that I like.'

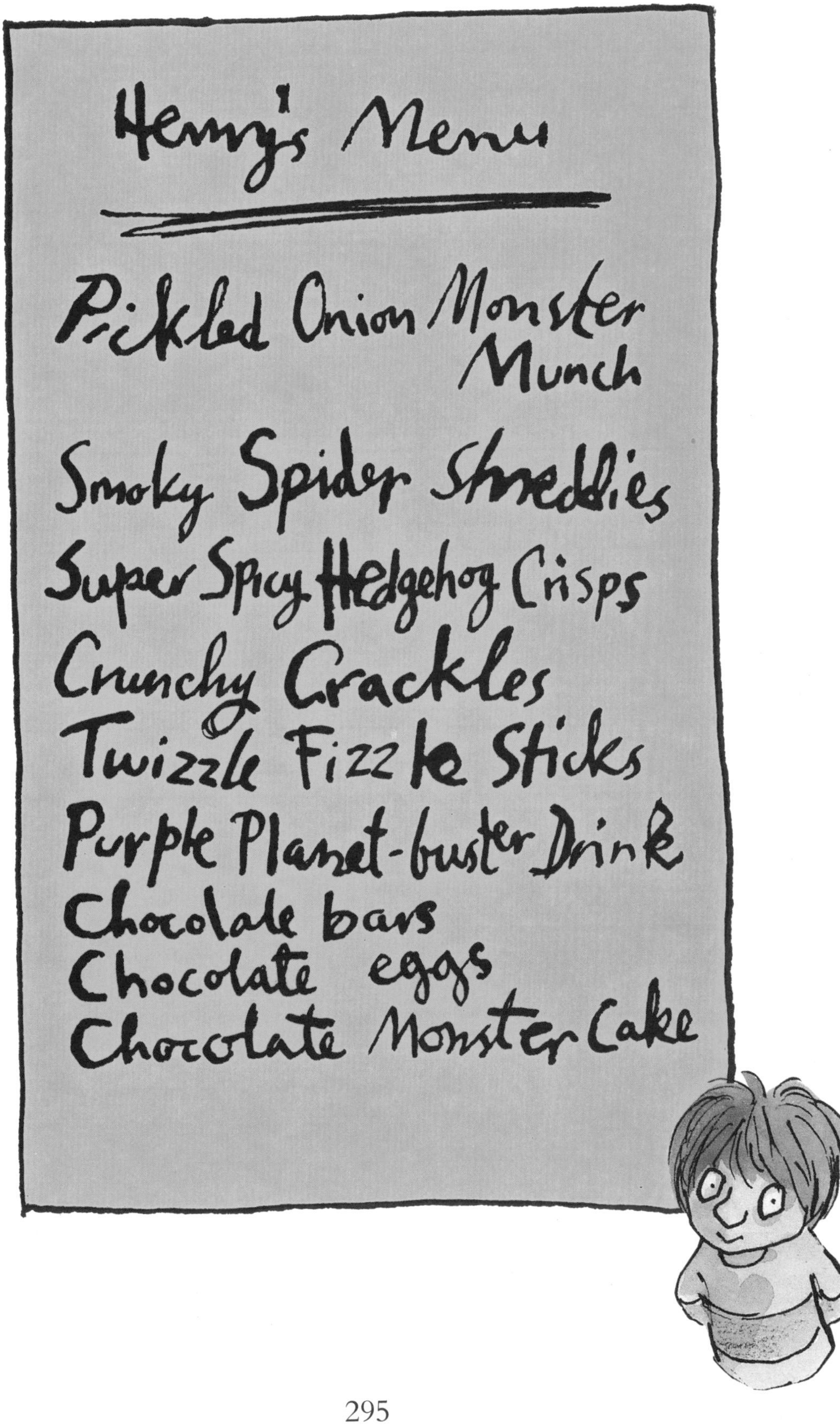

Henry's Menu

Pickled Onion Monster Munch

Smoky Spider Shreddies

Super Spicy Hedgehog Crisps

Crunchy Crackles

Twizzle Fizzle Sticks

Purple Planet-buster Drink

Chocolate bars

Chocolate eggs

Chocolate Monster Cake

'You can't just have junk food,' said Mum.

'It's not junk food,' said Henry. 'Crisps are made from potatoes, and Monster Munch has onions – that's two vegetables.'

'Henry . . .' said Mum. She looked fierce.

Henry looked at his menu. Then he added, in small letters at the bottom:

peanut butter sandwiches

'But only in the middle of the table,' said Henry. 'So no one has to eat them who doesn't want them.'

'All right,' said Mum. Years of fighting with Henry about his parties had worn her down.

'And Peter's not coming,' said Henry.

'What?!' said Perfect Peter, looking up from polishing his shoes.

'Peter is your brother. Of course he's invited.'

Henry scowled.

'But he'll ruin everything.'

'No Peter, no party,' said Mum.

Henry pretended he was a fire-breathing dragon.

'Owww!' shrieked Peter.

'Don't be horrid, Henry!' yelled Mum.

'All right,' said Henry. 'He can come. But you'd better keep out of my way,' he hissed at Peter.

'Mum!' wailed Peter. 'Henry's being mean to me.

'Stop it, Henry,' said Mum.

Henry decided to change the subject fast.

'What about party bags?' said Henry. 'I want everyone to have Slime, and loads and loads and loads of sweets! Dirt Balls, Nose Pickers and Foam Teeth are the best.'

'We'll see,' said Mum. She looked at the calendar. Only two more days. Soon it would be over.

Henry's birthday arrived at last.

'Happy birthday, Henry!' said Mum.

'Happy birthday, Henry!' said Dad.

'Happy birthday, Henry!' said Peter.

'Where are my presents?' said Henry.

Dad pointed. Horrid Henry attacked the pile.

Mum and Dad had given him a *First Encyclopedia,*

Scrabble, a fountain pen, a hand-knitted cardigan, a globe, and three sets of vests and pants.

'Oh,' said Henry. He pushed the dreadful presents aside.

'Anything else?' he asked hopefully. Maybe they were keeping the super soaker for last.

'I've got a present for you,' said Peter. 'I chose it myself.'

Henry tore off the wrapping paper. It was a tapestry kit.

'Yuck!' said Henry.

'I'll have it if you don't want it,' said Peter.

'No!' said Henry, snatching up the kit.

'Wasn't it a great idea to have Henry's party at Lazer Zap?' said Dad.

'Yes,' said Mum. 'No mess, no fuss.'

They smiled at each other.

Ring ring.

Dad answered the phone. It was the Lazer Zap lady.

'Hello! I was just ringing to check the birthday boy's name,' she said. 'We like to announce it over our loudspeaker during the party.'

Dad gave Henry's name.

A terrible scream came from the other end of the phone. Dad held the receiver away from his ear.

The shrieking and screaming continued.

'Hmmmn,' said Dad. 'I see. Thank you.'

Dad hung up. He looked pale.

'Henry!'

'Yeah?'

'Is it true that you wrecked the place when you went to Lazer Zap with Toby?' said Dad.

'No!' said Henry. He tried to look harmless.

'And trampled on several children?'

'No!' said Henry.

'Yes you did,' said Perfect Peter. 'And what about all the lasers you broke?'

'What lasers?' said Henry.

'And the slime you put in the space suits?' said Peter.

'That wasn't me, telltale,' shrieked Henry. 'What about my party?'

'I'm afraid Lazer Zap have banned you,' said Dad.

'But what about Henry's party?' said Mum. She looked pale.

'But what about my party?!' wailed Henry. 'I want to go to Lazer Zap!'

'Never mind,' said Dad brightly. 'I know lots of good games.'

Ding dong.

It was the first guest, Sour Susan. She held a large present.

Henry snatched the package.

It was a pad of paper and some felt tip pens.

'How lovely,' said Mum. 'What do you say, Henry?'

'I've already got that,' said Henry.

'Henry!' said Mum. 'Don't be horrid!'

I don't care, thought Henry. This was the worst day of his life.

Ding dong.

It was the second guest, Anxious Andrew. He held a tiny present.

Henry snatched the package.

'It's awfully small,' said Henry, tearing off the wrapping. 'And it smells.'

It was a box of animal soaps.

'How super,' said Dad. 'What do you say, Henry?'

'Ugghhh!' said Henry.

'Henry!' said Dad. 'Don't be horrid.'

Henry stuck out his lower lip.

'It's my party and I'll do what I want,' muttered Henry.

'Watch your step, young man,' said Dad.

Henry stuck out his tongue behind Dad's back.

More guests arrived.

Lazy Linda gave him a 'Read and Listen Cassette of Favourite Fairy Tales: Cinderella, Snow White and Sleeping Beauty'.

'Fabulous,' said Mum.

'Yuck!' said Henry.

Clever Clare handed him a square package.

Henry held it by the corners.

'It's a book,' he groaned.

'My favourite present!' said Peter.

'Wonderful,' said Mum. 'What is it?'

Henry unwrapped it slowly.

'*Cook Your Own Healthy Nutritious Food.*'

'Great!' said Perfect Peter. 'Can I borrow it?'

'NO!' screamed Henry. Then he threw the book on the floor and stomped on it.

'Henry!' hissed Mum. 'I'm warning you. When someone gives you a present you say thank you.'

Rude Ralph was the last to arrive.

He handed Henry a long rectangular package wrapped in newspaper.

It was a Super Soaker 2000 water blaster.

'Oh,' said Mum.

'Put it away,' said Dad.

'Thank you, Ralph,' beamed Henry. 'Just what I wanted.'

'Let's start with Pass the Parcel,' said Dad.

'I hate Pass the Parcel,' said Horrid Henry. What a horrible party this was.

'I love Pass the Parcel,' said Perfect Peter.

'I don't want to play,' said Sour Susan.

'When do we eat?' said Greedy Graham.

Dad started the music.

'Pass the parcel, William,' said Dad.

'No!' shrieked William. 'It's mine!'

'But the music is still playing,' said Dad.

William burst into tears.

Horrid Henry tried to snatch the parcel.

Dad stopped the music.

William stopped crying instantly and tore off the wrapping.

'A granola bar,' he said.

'That's a terrible prize,' said Rude Ralph.

'Is it my turn yet?' said Anxious Andrew.

'When do we eat?' said Greedy Graham.

'I hate Pass the Parcel,' screamed Henry. 'I want to play something else.'

'Musical Statues!' announced Mum brightly.

'You're out, Henry,' said Dad. 'You moved.'

'I didn't,' said Henry.

'Yes you did,' said Toby.

'No I didn't,' said Henry. 'I'm not leaving.'

'That's not fair,' shrieked Sour Susan.

'I'm not playing,' whined Dizzy Dave.

'I'm tired,' sulked Lazy Linda.

'I hate Musical Statues,' moaned Moody Margaret.

'Where's my prize?' demanded Rude Ralph.

'A bookmark?' said Ralph. 'That's it?'

'Tea time!' said Dad.

The children pushed and shoved their way to the table, grabbing and snatching at the food.

'I hate fizzy drinks,' said Tough Toby.

'I feel sick,' said Greedy Graham.

'Where are the carrot sticks?' said Perfect Peter.

Horrid Henry sat at the head of the table.

He didn't feel like throwing food at Clare.

He didn't feel like rampaging with Toby and Ralph.

He didn't even feel like kicking Peter.

He wanted to be at Lazer Zap.

Then Henry had a wonderful, spectacular idea. He got up and sneaked out of the room.

'Party bags,' said Dad.

'What's in them?' said Tough Toby.

'Seedlings,' said Mum.

'Where are the sweets?' said Greedy Graham.

'This is the worst party bag I've ever had,' said Rude Ralph.

There was a noise outside.

Then Henry burst into the kitchen, supersoaker in hand.

'ZAP! ZAP! ZAP!' shrieked Henry, drenching everyone with water. 'Ha! Ha! Gotcha!'

Splat went the cake.

Splash went the drinks.

'EEEEEEEEEEEEEKKK!' shrieked the sopping wet children.

'HENRY!!!!!' yelled Mum and Dad.

'YOU HORRID BOY!' yelled Mum. Water dripped from her hair. 'GO TO YOUR ROOM!'

'THIS IS YOUR LAST PARTY EVER!' yelled Dad. Water dripped from his clothes.

But Henry didn't care. They said that every year.

STAR CHART

Henry.	
Monday	
Tuesday	
Wednesday	
Thursday	★ ← for putting fork in dishwasher
Friday	
Saturday	
Sunday	

Peter.	
Monday	★ ★ ★ ★
Tuesday	★ ★ ★ ★ ★
Wednesday	★ ★ ★ ★
Thursday	★ ★ ★ ★
Friday	★ ★ ★ ★ ★
Saturday	★ ★ ★ ★
Sunday	★ ★ ★ ★ ★ ★

Dear Mum and Dad

NO thank you for the vests, socks and books.

BLEUCCCCK.

Why do I always get such yucky presents.

£10 is FAR too little.

Henry

HORRID HENRY'S THANK YOU LETTER

hh! This was the life! A sofa, a telly, a bag of crisps.
Horrid Henry sighed happily.

'Henry!' shouted Mum from the kitchen. 'Are you watching TV?'

Henry blocked his ears. Nothing was going to interrupt his new favourite TV programme, *Terminator Gladiator*.

'Answer me, Henry!' shouted Mum. 'Have you written your Christmas thank you letters?'

'NO!' bellowed Henry.

'Why not?' screamed Mum.

'Because I haven't,' said Henry. 'I'm busy.' Couldn't she leave him alone for two seconds?

Mum marched into the room and switched off the TV.

'Hey!' said Henry. 'I'm watching *Terminator Gladiator*.'

'Too bad,' said Mum. 'I told you, no TV until you've written your thank you letters.'

'It's not fair!' wailed Henry.

'I've written all *my* thank you letters,' said Perfect Peter.

'Well done, Peter,' said Mum. 'Thank goodness *one* of my children has good manners.'

Peter smiled modestly. 'I always write mine the moment I unwrap a present. I'm a good boy, aren't I?'

'The best,' said Mum.

'Oh, shut up, Peter,' snarled Henry.

'Mum! Henry told me to shut up!' said Peter.

'Stop being horrid, Henry. You will write to Aunt Ruby, Great-Aunt Greta and Grandma now.'

'Now?' moaned Henry. 'Can't I do it later?'

'When's later?' said Dad.

'Later!' said Henry. Why wouldn't they stop nagging him about those stupid letters?

Horrid Henry hated writing thank you letters. Why should he waste his precious time saying thank you for presents? Time he could be spending reading comics, or watching TV. But no. He would barely unwrap a present before Mum started nagging. She even expected him to write to Great-Aunt Greta and thank her for the Baby Poopie Pants doll. Great-Aunt Greta for one did not deserve a thank you letter.

This year Aunt Ruby had sent him a hideous lime green cardigan. Why should he thank her for that?

True, Grandma had given him £15, which was great. But then Mum had to spoil it by making him write her a letter too. Henry hated writing letters for nice presents every bit as much as he hated writing them for horrible ones.

'You have to write thank you letters,' said Dad.

'But why?' said Henry.

'Because it's polite,' said Dad.

'Because people have spent time and money on you,' said Mum.

So what? thought Horrid Henry. Grown-ups had loads of time to do whatever they wanted. No one told them, stop watching TV and write a thank you letter. Oh no. They could do it whenever they felt like it. Or not even do it at all.

And adults had tons of money compared to him. Why shouldn't they spend it buying him presents?

'All you have to do is write one page,' said Dad. 'What's the big deal?'

Henry stared at him. Did Dad have no idea how long it would take him to write one whole page? Hours and hours and hours.

'You're the meanest, most horrible parents in the world and I hate you!' shrieked Horrid Henry.

'Go to your room, Henry!' shouted Dad.

'And don't come down until you've written those letters,' shouted Mum. 'I am sick and tired of arguing about this.'

Horrid Henry stomped upstairs.

Well, no way was he writing any thank you letters. He'd rather starve. He'd rather die. He'd stay in his room for a month. A year. One day Mum and Dad would come up to check on him and all they'd find would be a few bones. Then they'd be sorry.

Actually, knowing them, they'd probably just moan about the mess. And then Peter would be all happy because he'd get Henry's room and Henry's room was bigger.

Well, no way would he give them the satisfaction. All right, thought Horrid Henry. Dad said to write one page. Henry would write one page. In his biggest, most gigantic handwriting, Henry wrote:

Dear Aunt Ruby,
Thank you
for the
present.

Henry

That certainly filled a whole page, thought Horrid
Henry.

Mum came into the room.

'Have you written your letters yet?'

'Yes,' lied Henry.

Mum glanced over his shoulder.

'Henry!' said Mum. 'That is not a proper thank you letter.'

'Yes it is,' snarled Henry. 'Dad said to write one page so I wrote one page.'

'Write five sentences,' said Mum.

Five sentences? Five whole sentences? It was completely impossible for anyone to write so much. His hand would fall off.

'That's way too much,' wailed Henry.

'No TV until you write your letters,' said Mum, leaving the room.

Horrid Henry stuck out his tongue. He had the meanest, most horrible parents in the world. When he was King any parent who even whispered the words 'thank you letter' would get fed to the crocodiles.

They wanted five sentences? He'd give them five sentences. Henry picked up his pencil and scrawled:

Dear Aunt Ruby,
No thank you for the horrible present. It is the worst present I have ever had. Anyway, didn't some old Roman say it was better to give than to receive? So in fact, you should be writing me a thank you letter.
Henry
P.S. Next time just send money.

There! Five whole sentences. Perfect, thought Horrid Henry. Mum said he had to write a five-sentence thank you letter. She never said it had to be a *nice* thank you letter. Suddenly Henry felt quite cheerful. He folded the letter and popped it in the stamped envelope Mum had given him.

One down. Two to go.

In fact, Aunt Ruby's no thank you letter would do just fine for Great-Aunt Greta. He'd just substitute Great-Aunt Greta's name for Aunt Ruby's and copy the rest.

Bingo. Another letter was done.

Now, Grandma. She *had* sent money so he'd have to write something nice.

'Thank you for the money, blah blah blah, best present I've ever received, blah blah blah, next year send more money, £15 isn't very much, Ralph got £20 from *his* grandma, blah blah blah.'

What a waste, thought Horrid Henry as he signed it and put it in the envelope, to spend so much time on a letter, only to have to write the same old thing all over again next year.

And then suddenly Horrid Henry had a wonderful, spectacular idea. Why had he never thought of this before? He would be rich, rich, rich. 'There goes money-bags Henry,' kids would whisper enviously, as he swaggered down the street, followed by Peter lugging a hundred videos for Henry to watch in his

mansion on one of his twenty-eight giant TVs. Mum
and Dad and Peter would be living in their hovel
somewhere, and if they were very, very nice to him
Henry *might* let them watch one of his smaller TVs for
fifteen minutes or so once a month.

Henry was going to start a business. A business
guaranteed to make him rich.

'Step right up, step right up,' said Horrid Henry. He
was wearing a sign saying: 'HENRY'S THANK YOU
LETTERS: Personal letters written just for you.' A
small crowd of children gathered round him.

'I'll write all your thank you letters for you,' said
Henry. 'All you have to do is to give me a stamped,
addressed envelope and tell me what present you got.

I'll do the rest.'

'How much for a thank you letter?' asked Kung-Fu Kate.

'A pound,' said Henry.

'No way,' said Greedy Graham.

'99p,' said Henry.

'Forget it,' said Lazy Linda.

'OK, 50p,' said Henry. 'And two for 75p.'

'Done,' said Linda.

Henry opened his notebook. 'And what were the presents?' he asked. Linda made a face. 'Handkerchiefs,' she spat. 'And a bookmark.'

'I can do a "no thank you" letter,' said Henry. 'I'm very good at those.' Linda considered.

'Tempting,' she said, 'but then mean Uncle John won't send something better next time.'

Business was brisk. Dave bought three. Ralph bought four 'no thank you's. Even Moody Margaret bought one. Whoopee, thought Horrid Henry. His pockets were jingle-jangling with cash. Now all he had to do was to write seventeen letters. Henry tried not to think about that.

The moment he got home from school Henry went straight to his room. Right, to work, thought Henry. His heart sank as he looked at the blank pages. All those letters! He would be here for weeks. Why had he ever set up a letter-writing business?

But then Horrid Henry thought. True, he'd promised a personal letter but how would Linda's aunt ever find out that Margaret's granny had received the same one? She wouldn't! If he used the computer, it would be a cinch. And it would be a letter sent personally, thought Henry, because I am a person and I will personally print it out and send it. All he'd have to do was to write the names at the top and to sign them. Easy-peasy lemon squeezy.

Then again, all that signing. And writing all those names at the top. And separating the thank you letters from the no thank you ones.

Maybe there was a better way.

Horrid Henry sat down at the computer and typed:

Dear Sir or Madam,

That should cover everyone, thought Henry, and I won't have to write anyone's name.

Thank you/No thank you for the
a) wonderful
b) horrible
c) disgusting
present. I really loved it/hated it. In fact, it is the best present/worst present I have ever received. I played with it/broke it/ate it/spent it/threw it in the bin straight away. Next time just send lots of money.
Best wishes/worst wishes

Now, how to sign it? Aha, thought Henry.

Your friend or relative.

Perfect, thought Horrid Henry. Sir or Madam knows whether they deserve a thank you or a no thank you letter. Let them do some work for a change and tick the correct answers.

Out spewed seventeen letters. It only took a moment to stuff them in the envelopes. He'd pop the letters in the postbox on the way to school.

Had an easier way to become a millionaire ever been invented? thought Horrid Henry, as he turned on the telly.

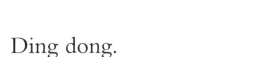

Ding dong.

It was two weeks after Henry set up 'Henry's Thank You Letters'.

Horrid Henry opened the door.

A group of Henry's customers stood there, waving pieces of paper and shouting.

'My granny sent the letter back and now I can't watch TV for a week,' wailed Moody Margaret.

'I'm grounded!' screamed Aerobic Al.

'I have to go swimming!' screamed Lazy Linda.

'No sweets!' yelped Greedy Graham.

'No pocket money!' screamed Rude Ralph.

'And it's all your fault!' they shouted.

Horrid Henry glared at his angry customers. He was outraged. After all his hard work, *this* was the thanks he got?

'Too bad!' said Horrid Henry as he slammed the door. Honestly, there was no pleasing some people.

'Henry,' said Mum. 'I just had the strangest phone call from Aunt Ruby . . .'

Holiday Snaps

JOKES NOT TO TELL AUNT RUBY

MUM: Henry! I've just had
the strangest call from Aunt Ruby . . .
HENRY: **Hide!**

What do you call an aunt on the toilet?
Lou Lou.

What do you call an aunt who falls off the toilet?
Lou Roll.

Why do you put your aunt in the fridge?
To make Auntie-freeze.

Has your aunt caught up with you yet?
No, but when she does I'm going to need a lot of Auntie-septic.

How do you make anti-freeze?
Hide her nightie.

How can you tell if Aunt Ruby's been to visit?
She's still in the house.

MUM: Henry, we're having Aunt Ruby for lunch this
Sunday.
HENRY: **Can't we have roast beef instead?**

MUM: Henry! Why did you put a slug in
Aunt Ruby's bed?
HENRY: **I couldn't find
a snake.**

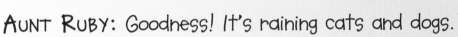

AUNT RUBY: Goodness! It's raining cats and dogs.
HENRY: **I know. I nearly stepped in a
poodle.**

AUNT RUBY: Well, Henry,
I'm leaving tomorrow.
Are you sorry?

HENRY: Oh yes,
Aunt Ruby,
I thought you were
leaving
today.

Not
Suitable
for
Aunts

Dear Father Chrismas
I don't understand why
you didn't bring me the
Robomatic Supersonic Space
Howler I askd for.
I wrote it in HUGE letters.
Can't you read ?
It had better not happen
again .
You have been Warned.
Henry

HORRID HENRY'S HOLIDAY

Horrid Henry hated holidays.

Henry's idea of a super holiday was sitting on the sofa eating crisps and watching TV.

Unfortunately, his parents usually had other plans.

Once they took him to see some castles. But there were no castles. There were only piles of stones and broken walls.

'Never again,' said Henry.

The next year he had to go to a lot of museums.

'Never again,' said Mum and Dad.

Last year they went to the seaside.

'The sun is too hot,' Henry whined.

'The water is too cold,' Henry whinged.

'The food is yucky,' Henry grumbled.

'The bed is lumpy,' Henry moaned.

This year they decided to try something different.

'We're going camping in France,' said Henry's parents.

'Hooray!' said Henry.

'You're happy, Henry?' said Mum. Henry had never been happy about any holiday plans before.

'Oh yes,' said Henry. Finally, finally, they were doing something good.

Henry knew all about camping from Moody Margaret. Margaret had been camping with her family. They had stayed in a big tent with comfy beds, a fridge, a cooker, a loo, a shower, a heated swimming pool, a disco and a great big giant TV with fifty-seven channels.

'Oh boy!' said Horrid Henry.

'Bonjour!' said Perfect Peter.

The great day arrived at last. Horrid Henry, Perfect Peter, Mum and Dad boarded the ferry for France.

Henry and Peter had never been on a boat before.

Henry jumped on and off the seats.

Peter did a lovely drawing.

The boat went up and down and up and down.

Henry ran back and forth between the aisles.

Peter pasted stickers in his notebook.

The boat went up and down and up and down.

Henry sat on a revolving chair and spun round.

Peter played with his puppets.

334

The boat went up and down and up and down.

Then Henry and Peter ate a big greasy lunch of sausages and chips in the café.

The boat went up and down, and up and down, and up and down.

Henry began to feel queasy.

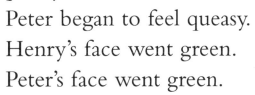

Peter began to feel queasy.

Henry's face went green.

Peter's face went green.

'I think I'm going to be sick,' said Henry, and threw up all over Mum.

'I think I'm going to be –' said Peter, and threw up all over Dad.

'Oh no,' said Mum.

'Never mind,' said Dad. 'I just know this will be our best holiday ever.'

Finally, the boat arrived in France.

After driving and driving and driving they reached the campsite.

It was even better than Henry's dreams. The tents were as big as houses. Henry heard the happy sound of TVs blaring, music playing, and children splashing and shrieking. The sun shone. The sky was blue.

'Wow, this looks great,' said Henry.

But the car drove on.

'Stop!' said Henry. 'You've gone too far.'

'We're not staying in that awful place,' said Dad.

They drove on.

'Here's our campsite,' said Dad. 'A *real* campsite!'

Henry stared at the bare rocky ground under the cloudy grey sky.

There were three small tents flapping in the wind. There was a single tap. There were a few trees. There was nothing else.

'It's wonderful!' said Mum.

'It's wonderful!' said Peter.

'But where's the TV?' said Henry.

'No TV here, thank goodness,' said Mum. 'We've got books.'

'But where are the beds?' said Henry.

'No beds here, thank goodness,' said Dad. 'We've got sleeping bags.'

'But where's the pool?' said Henry.

'No pool,' said Dad. '*We'll* swim in the river.'

'Where's the toilet?' said Peter.

Dad pointed at a distant cubicle. Three people stood waiting.

'All the way over there?' said Peter. 'I'm not complaining,' he added quickly.

Mum and Dad unpacked the car. Henry stood and scowled.

'Who wants to help put up the tent?' asked Mum.

'I do!' said Dad.

'I do!' said Peter.

Henry was horrified. 'We have to put up our own tent?'

'Of course,' said Mum.

'I don't like it here,' said Henry. 'I want to go camping in the other place.'

'That's not camping,' said Dad. 'Those tents have beds in them. And loos. And showers. And fridges. And cookers, and TVs. Horrible.' Dad shuddered.

'Horrible,' said Peter.

'And we have such a lovely snug tent here,' said Mum. 'Nothing modern – just wooden pegs and poles.'

'Well, I want to stay there,' said Henry.

'We're staying here,' said Dad.

'NO!' screamed Henry.

'YES!' screamed Dad.

I am sorry to say that Henry then had the longest, loudest, noisiest, shrillest, most horrible tantrum you can imagine.

Did you think that a horrid boy like Henry would like nothing better than sleeping on hard rocky ground in a soggy sleeping bag without a pillow?

You thought wrong.

Henry liked comfy beds.

Henry liked crisp sheets.

Henry liked hot baths.

Henry liked microwave dinners, TV, and noise.

He did not like cold showers, fresh air, and quiet.

Far off in the distance the sweet sound of loud music drifted towards them.

'Aren't you glad we're not staying in that awful noisy place?' said Dad.

'Oh yes,' said Mum.

'Oh yes,' said Perfect Peter.

Henry pretended he was a bulldozer come to knock down tents and squash campers.

'Henry, don't barge into the tent!' yelled Dad.

Henry pretended he was a hungry Tyrannosaurus Rex.

'OW!' shrieked Peter.

'Henry, don't be horrid!' yelled Mum.

She looked up at the dark cloudy sky.

'It's going to rain,' said Mum.

'Don't worry,' said Dad. 'It never rains when I'm camping.'

'The boys and I will go and collect some more firewood,' said Mum.

'I'm not moving,' said Horrid Henry.

While Dad made a campire, Henry played his boom-box as loud as he could, stomping in time to the terrible music of the Killer Boy Rats.

'Henry, turn that noise down this minute,' said Dad.

Henry pretended not to hear.

'HENRY!' yelled Dad. 'TURN THAT DOWN!'

Henry turned the volume down the teeniest tiniest fraction.

The terrible sounds of the Killer Boy Rats continued to boom over the quiet campsite.

Campers emerged from their tents and shook their fists. Dad switched off Henry's tape player.

'Anything wrong, Dad?' asked Henry, in his sweetest voice.

'No,' said Dad.

Mum and Peter returned carrying armfuls of firewood.

It started to drizzle.

'This is fun,' said Mum, slapping a mosquito.

'Isn't it?' said Dad. He was heating up some tins of baked beans.

The drizzle turned into a downpour.

The wind blew.

The campfire hissed, and went out.

'Never mind,' said Dad brightly. 'We'll eat our baked beans cold.'

Mum was snoring.

Dad was snoring.

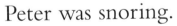

Peter was snoring.

Henry tossed and turned. But whichever way he turned in his damp sleeping bag, he seemed to be lying on sharp, pointy stones.

Above him, mosquitoes whined.

I'll never get to sleep, he thought, kicking Peter. How am I going to bear this for fourteen days?

Around four o'clock on Day Five the family huddled inside the cold, damp, smelly tent listening to the howling wind and the pouring rain.

'Time for a walk!' said Dad.

'Great idea!' said Mum, sneezing. 'I'll get the boots.'

'Great idea!' said Peter, sneezing. 'I'll get the macs.'

'But it's pouring outside,' said Henry.

'So?' said Dad. 'What better time to go for a walk?'

'I'm not coming,' said Horrid Henry.

'I am,' said Perfect Peter. 'I don't mind the rain.'

Dad poked his head outside the tent.

'The rain has stopped,' he said. 'I'll remake the fire.'

'I'm not coming,' said Henry.

'We need more firewood,' said Dad. 'Henry can stay here and collect some. And make sure it's dry.'

Henry poked his head outside the tent. The rain had stopped, but the sky was still cloudy. The fire spat.

I won't go, thought Henry. The forest will be all muddy and wet.

He looked round to see if there was any wood closer to home.

That was when he saw the thick, dry wooden pegs holding up all the tents.

Henry looked to the left.

Henry looked to the right.

No one was around.

If I just take a few pegs from each tent, he thought, they'll never be missed.

When Mum and Dad came back they were delighted.

'What a lovely roaring fire,' said Mum.

'Clever you to find some dry wood,' said Dad.

The wind blew.

Henry dreamed he was floating in a cold river, floating, floating, floating.

He woke up. He shook his head. He *was* floating. The tent was filled with cold muddy water.

Then the tent collapsed on top of them.

Henry, Peter, Mum and Dad stood outside in the rain and stared at the river of water gushing through their collapsed tent.

All round them soaking wet campers were staring at their collapsed tents.

Peter sneezed.

Mum sneezed.

Dad sneezed.

Henry coughed, choked, spluttered and sneezed.

'I don't understand it,' said Dad. 'This tent *never* collapses.'

'What are we going to do?' said Mum.

'I know,' said Henry. 'I've got a very good idea.'

Two hours later Mum, Dad, Henry and Peter were sitting on a sofa-bed inside a tent as big as a house, eating crisps and watching TV.

The sun was shining. The sky was blue.

'Now this is what I call a holiday!' said Henry.

HORRID HENRY'S HOME FACT FILE

Parents
Mum and Dad

Brothers
One horrible younger brother, Perfect Peter

Cousins
Stuck-up Steve
Prissy Polly
Pimply Paul
Vomiting Vera

Aunts
Rich Aunt Ruby
Great-Aunt Greta

Grandparents
Grandma
Grandpa

Pets
Fang (hamster)
Fluffy (cat)

Catchphrase
Out of my way, worm!

Hobbies
Eating sweets
Collecting gizmos

Pocket money
50p per week
(much too little)

Favourite sweets
Big Boppers
Nose Pickers
Dirt Balls

Worst sweets
None

Favourite food
Crisps
Chocolate
Pizza

Worst food
Vegetables
Muesli

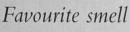

Favourite smell
Pancakes

Favourite places
Whopper Whoopee
Gobble and Go
Toy Heaven

Favourite TV programmes
Gross-Out
Rapper Zapper
Mutant Max
Terminator Gladiator
Hog House

Worst TV programmes

Manners with Maggie
Daffy and her Dancing Daisies

Favourite pop groups

Driller Cannibals
Killer Boy Rats

Favourite computer games

Intergalactic Killer Robots
Snake Masters Revenge III

Worst computer games

Be a Spelling Champion
Virtual Classroom
Whoopee for Numbers

Best present
Money

Worst present
Frilly pink lacy underpants

Worst punishment
No TV for a week

Greatest ambition
To be crowned King Henry the Horrible